P9-DFO-645

SO
YOUNG
TO
DIE

The Story of Hannah Senesh

St. Michael School
1203 E. 10th Ave.
Olympia, WA 98501

Other Scholastic biographies
you will enjoy:

Thomas Jefferson: Man with a Vision
by Ruth Crisman

Faithful Friend: The Story of Florence Nightingale
by Beatrice Siegel

Colin Powell: A Biography
by Jim Haskins

Nelson Mandela: "No Easy Walk to Freedom"
by Barry Denenberg

Jesse Jackson: A Biography
by Patricia C. McKissack

Christopher Columbus: Admiral of the Ocean Sea
by Jim Haskins

SO YOUNG TO DIE

The Story of Hannah Senesh

Candice F. Ransom

SCHOLASTIC INC.
New York Toronto London Auckland Sydney

Diary excerpts are taken from *Hannah Senesh: Her Life and Diary* by Hannah Senesh, translated by Marta Cohn. Copyright © 1971 by Nigel Marsh. Reprinted by permission of Schocken Books, published by Pantheon Books, a division of Random House Inc. and Vallentine Mitchell and Co., Ltd.

Photo Credits

Frontispiece courtesy of George Senesh.
Insert: Photos 1, 2, 3, 4, 5, and 12 courtesy of George Senesh. Photos 6, 7, and 10 courtesy of Yad Vashem, Jerusalem. Photos 8 and 11, courtesy of Beit Chanah Senesh — Sdot-Yam. Photo 9 courtesy of Ghetto Fighters' House. Photo 13 courtesy of the Kibbutz Sdot-Yam. Photo 14 courtesy of the Government Press Office, State of Israel.

If you purchased this book without a cover, you should be aware that this book is stolen property. It was reported as "unsold and destroyed" to the publisher, and neither the author nor the publisher has received any payment for this "stripped book."

No part of this publication may be reproduced in whole or in part, or stored in a retrieval system, or transmitted in any form or by any means, electronic, mechanical, photocopying, recording, or otherwise, without written permission of the publisher. For information regarding permission, write to Scholastic Inc., 730 Broadway, New York, NY 10003.

ISBN 0-590-44677-0

Copyright © 1993 by Candice F. Ransom.
All rights reserved. Published by Scholastic Inc.

12 11 10 9 8 7 6 5 4   3 4 5 6 7 8/9

Printed in the U.S.A.   40

First Scholastic printing, March 1993

Contents

To Die . . .

To die . . . so young to die . . . no, no, not I.
I love the warm sunny skies,
Light, songs, shining eyes.
I want no war, no battle cry —
No, no . . . Not I.
But if it must be that I live today
With blood and death on every hand,
Praised be He for the grace, I'll say
To live, if I should die this day . . .
Upon your soil, my home, my land.

—Nahalal, 1941

Prologue

The cell was cold now that it was November. She had only a thin dress to ward off the chill from the stone walls and floor, a dampness that seemed to drip into her very bones.

The prison was nearly empty. She could hear the hurrying footsteps and hoarse echoing cries of the guards. She smelled the acrid smoke from the furnaces but did not know the guards were burning prison records.

Outside Allied bombs hailed on the city, rattling her windowpanes. Cannon fire marked the steady progress of the Red Army, knocking at the gates of Budapest. Who would get there first, the Allies or the Russians? Would they arrive in time to save the prisoners from starvation?

She was hungry all the time. And lonely. She hadn't seen her mother since the trial. No one came to see her, except the jailor to bring her daily ration of watered-down soup. She didn't blame her mother for not coming — it was too dangerous.

This dismal prison cell was so different from the Land. The markets in Haifa were a feast for the eyes. Pyramids of oranges, capturing gold from the sun, baskets of tomatoes, olives, sweet dates . . .

Date palms grew in the valley called the Emek, their tops heavy with bunches of ruby-red fruit against a deep blue sky. A daytime full moon, round as a grapefruit, changed from pale white to silver as the sun took over the sky. The sunsets were glorious in the Land; mingling purples and pinks made a sharp contrast to the monotonous desert hues. Mount Tabor rose majestically from the cypress-covered foothills of Jezreel, the mountains where Deborah had answered the long-ago call of the Israelites, and stood fast against the chariot warriors of Sisera.

The images faded like the last light in an empty room. Unlike Deborah, Hannah Senesh would not conquer an army. She had surrendered Palestine to return to Hungary, her former homeland. Now both countries were lost to her.

Everything was lost.

BRIEF
AND HURTLING DAYS
1921–1939

1
Awakening

Hannah Senesh began her diary shortly after her thirteenth birthday, when she came back from visiting her cousin Evi in Dombovar. Mr. Toth, the schoolmaster, urged her to keep a journal. A diary was a good place to preserve memories, he'd added, and if her house ever caught fire, the diary would be the first thing she'd save.

Her diary wasn't worth rescuing from a fire, at least not yet. It wasn't anything fancy, just a blank, blue-covered exercise book like the ones she used at school. She had been writing poetry for years, but needed a place to voice her innermost thoughts, along with recording her numerous activities.

Her earliest entries were unremarkable, giving no indication of the extraordinary strength and powerful convictions she would later exhibit.

Her first entry was dated September 7, 1934:

This morning we visited Daddy's grave. How sad that we had to become acquainted with the cemetery so early in life.

Hannah had loved her father, Bela Senesh, a great deal. Sometimes she found it difficult to believe he had been gone for more than seven years. She wasn't quite six when he died. Her brother George was only seven.

Memories of the years her father was alive were sprinkled with magic. It was as if they all had been under a happy spell in those days. Bela Senesh had been a celebrated writer. He had written plays, novels, poems, and was a columnist for Budapest's main newspaper, *Pesti Hirlap*. His column was called "The Coalman" and was very witty, like his plays.

Hannah remembered her father as a warm, gentle man, tall and thin with a mustache and intelligent blue eyes. In the evenings their big house was always filled with friends of her father who laughed and talked about art and drama until long after Hannah was in bed. Her father wrote at night when the house was quiet, and did not get up until late in the mornings.

Bela was not well. A bout with rheumatic fever when he was a child had left him with a weak heart. He suspected he would not have the luxury of seeing old age and would have to do a lot of living in a short time. He hurried through life, marrying the beautiful Catherine Salzberger when they were both very young, and then working hard to become a successful writer.

The Seneshes lived in Rose Hill, a pretty, tree-lined neighborhood in Budapest, Hungary. In 1920, they had a son, George. A year later, on July 17, Hannah was born.

Hannah adored her father. In the mornings, she and George would pile into their father's bed. He would tell them stories he made up and Hungarian folktales about heroes on dangerous quests. Hannah listened intently. She loved to hear her father's stories.

Bela Senesh was full of surprises. For Hannah, days with him were like surprise presents waiting to be opened. He took her and George on walks throughout the city, pointing out the ornate Budapest Opera House and the Coronation Church with its soaring spire. He showed them the Millennium Memorial, the monument that marked the thousandth anniversary of the nation of Hungary. He took them sledding in the winter and treated them to pastries at one of the many coffeehouses where poets and artists gathered to discuss their work.

They strolled along the Danube, the river that divided the city into two parts, Buda and Pest. The two halves were united in 1872, and the city was then called Budapest. From Mount Gellert, on the Pest side of the river, Hannah could see Castle Hill, the site of the Royal Palace, the rolling hills of Buda, and the six bridges spanning the Danube.

She saw the cupola of Saint Stephen's Basilica. Hannah had heard the legend of Saint Stephen at a program at George's school. Vajk had been a heathen who was baptized Stephen by Bishop Gellert. Hannah enjoyed stories about ordinary people doing great deeds.

Bela Senesh sensed his time with his children was limited. He took Hannah and George to the zoo and the amusement park and gave afternoon parties just for them and their friends. At these parties, Bela entertained the children for hours with his stories.

And then one spring day in 1927, the parties and stories ended abruptly. Bela Senesh died in his sleep of a heart attack. The enchanted spell was broken.

Catherine Senesh became both father and mother to Hannah and George. Josephine, Catherine's mother, rounded out the household. Hannah called her grandmother Fini Mama.

Hannah was only six when she began writing poems, shortly after her father's death. Fini Mama wrote them down. Her earliest efforts reflected her grief:

> *I would like to be glad but don't know how*
> *No matter how I'd like to be*
> *No matter how I want to be*

In the fall of 1927, Hannah started school. She adjusted happily and made good grades, even though she didn't appear to study. After completing the four elementary grades, ten-year-old Hannah was ready for higher levels of education.

Although the family was Jewish, Catherine Senesh enrolled Hannah in a nearby well-respected Protestant girls' school. That year the school accepted Catholic and Jewish girls for the first time. However, Catholic students had to pay twice the tuition fees, and Jewish students were required to pay triple.

Hannah thrived in her new school. She had lots of friends and was always at the top of her class. She was not aware then that she was subject to prejudice because she was Jewish.

The Seneshes were Jews but wanted to be recognized as Hungarians first. Bela had changed his family name from "Schlesinger" to the more Hungarian-sounding "Senesh." They were faithful to their religion, but downplayed the role of religion in their everyday lives.

On his first day of school, a year before Hannah started, George was unable to answer when his teacher asked him his religion. Religious instruction was part of his school's program, but George didn't know how to answer his teacher. He had not heard much about religion at home. He was put into a Protestant class until his teacher checked his birth certificate and transferred him to the class for Jewish boys.

George ran home to tell his family this astonishing news. They were Jews! Hannah, only five at the time, had no idea they were Jewish either. Did it make any difference? Her brother told her things, like why they didn't have a Christmas tree at Christmas, and they realized there were differences between Jews and Gentiles.

At the end of Hannah's first year in the new school, her mother went to the principal.

Armed with Hannah's excellent report card, Catherine Senesh informed the principal that her daughter by rights should have a scholarship. Mrs. Senesh pointed out that instead, they were paying three times the standard tuition. Although she regarded the school highly, she was planning to enroll Hannah in a different school.

Immediately one of Hannah's favorite teachers spoke out. They wouldn't allow Hannah to leave, Catherine Senesh later reported in a record of her daughter's childhood. The teacher went on to say that Hannah was the school's finest student, popular with the students and trusted by the teachers. The other girls followed her example. They weren't even resentful when a teacher left the class in Hannah's care, an action that normally branded a student "teacher's pet." Hannah told the class stories, keeping them spellbound as her father once had done for her and George.

Hannah's tuition was lowered to twice the standard fee, the amount Catholic students were required to pay. Satisfied with that limited victory, Mrs. Senesh let her daughter stay in the school.

Hannah knew nothing of the inequality in her school's tuition policy. She even convinced her cousin Evi that she should transfer to her school. She continued to earn top marks and win prizes

10

for her scholastic abilities. Hannah believed everyone could do well and began coaching other girls when she was eleven. By the time she was thirteen, she was sought after as a tutor. She recorded her business dealing in her diary:

Today I finally reached an agreement with Maria's mother. I'm to coach Maria six hours a week. I will be paid fifteen *pengö* [six dollars and twenty-five cents] per month . . . I don't think any other girl in my class earns as much. Now I can pay for dancing and skating lessons with my own money. Perhaps I'll even buy a season ticket for the ice rink.

Although Hannah made excellent grades, she worried when report time came around. She imagined she would get a bad mark for neatness. But she worried for nothing — she received good marks in every subject, including neatness. Ever the perfectionist, Hannah looked for ways to improve herself. Even though she got an A in French, she wondered how she could do better.

Most of the time, though, Hananh had the usual concerns of a thirteen-year-old. Like any older brother, George teased her. She detailed one such incident in her diary:

George found my diary not long ago, and read the entire thing. I was furious because he constantly teased me about it. But last night he took a solemn oath never to mention it again.

Brother and sister disputes aside, she got along well with her brother. Their father's early death brought them closer together, as if they realized their family's diminishing number meant they would have to strive to find a place in the world. Hannah sorely missed the guidance her father would have provided them. She wrote wistfully in her journal:

> But I feel that even from beyond the grave Daddy is helping us, if in no other way than with his name. I don't think he could have left us a greater legacy.

Being the daughter of a famous playwright had its advantages. The Seneshes led a comfortable existence. They were not rich, but Mrs. Senesh employed a housekeeper, Rosika, who cooked and cleaned for them. Hannah did not even have to make her bed in the mornings.

Like most girls her age, Hannah fretted over her appearance. She was not beautiful and she knew it. She summed up her looks in her diary, viewing herself with the clear-eyed honesty that was her most enduring trait:

> I'm glad I've grown lately. I'm now five feet tall, and weigh just over seven stone [98 pounds]. I don't believe people think me a particularly pretty girl, but I hope I'll improve.

Her forehead was a bit too wide for her oval

face. But she had large eyes that seemed to change from green to blue, depending on her mood, and her dark brown hair was thick and curly. Her developing figure was cute — already her legs were her best feature. A photograph taken during this time showed Hannah gazing confidently into the lens. Her somewhat shy smile, though, contradicted this image. Outwardly, Hannah appeared to own the world. Inwardly, as her diary would later reflect, she was unsure of herself, uncertain of where she was going.

But at thirteen, she didn't worry about which direction she was headed in. She was busy with school, her friends, and family celebrations. During the Christmas season, when her school was closed for two weeks, she attended the opera with her family:

> Sunday we went . . . to hear *The Barber of Seville*. It was a beautiful performance . . .

She also listed the presents she received for Hanukkah that year. She got tickets to the opera from her mother, two pairs of stocking from one grandmother, a brooch from her other grandmother, dress fabric from her Aunt Ilus, handkerchiefs and ski stockings from her Aunt Irma, and three books.

Weeks passed without a word in her diary. Between school, the Ice Skating Club, and the Dance Circle, her days were full. In bed with the sniffles one Sunday shortly after the new year, she recorded her anxiety about an upcoming dance:

The Dance Circle will be held on the 26th. I am rather jittery about it, and wonder what it will be like. I have a lovely pink dress for the occasion.

Immersed in all her activities, Hannah was largely unaware of warnings on the horizon, hinting of the global disaster to come. She knew Adolf Hitler had become chancellor of Germany in 1933. Hitler was the leader of the Nazi Party that was now the ruling government. His gathering strength in Germany was like heat lightning, too distant to be considered much of a threat.

The previous November, Hannah and George had watched a parade to celebrate the fifteenth anniversary of Hungary's elected regent, Miklos Horthy. As the soldiers trooped down the boulevard, Hannah was impressed by their uniforms and military precision. But later she confided to her diary:

But what would become of them in war? Mother says the whole atmosphere is very warlike. It's a good thing George is still so young. Even so, God protect us from war. Why, the whole world would be practically wiped out.

But, like many people, Hannah wasn't overly bothered by what was happening in Europe. At that time, her future included her friends and doing the things she loved, like dancing and ice skating.

Near the end of the school term, Hannah and her classmates planned a reunion. They would meet in ten years and have a big party. They ordered rings with the date of the reunion, May 1, 1945.

The rings arrived just before school ended for the year. "Ten years from now!" she wrote in her diary. "What a long time! How many things can happen before then."

She did not know that by 1945 the whole world .would be turned upside down . . . and she would be dead.

2
The Approaching Storm

When school ended on June 15, Hannah boarded the two o'clock train. She had earned all A's on her report card, even in French, and she was eager to start her summer holiday. Judy, a friend from school, had invited her to spend a few weeks with her family at Lake Balaton.

Hannah loved the lakeside resort, though she felt a bit uncomfortable with Judy's family. As she later wrote in her diary, ". . . I certainly did not feel as much at home, as, for example, at Dombovar. Nor did I achieve a truly warm friendship with Judy." Perhaps seventeen days were too long to be constantly together.

She purposely left her diary home, afraid someone might discover it. Not that she had any deep dark secrets. Still, she didn't want anyone to read it.

Hannah did enjoy her talks with Judy's father. In the evenings, they discussed ideas that stimulated Hannah's active imagination, like the possibility of fate playing a hand in the direction of one's life. She agreed there might be something to astrology and spiritualism. Did destiny control her life or did she? It was an intriguing question.

Her mind constantly churned, with ideas, and passages she'd read in books, and snatches of poetry. She read Maeterlinck's *The Blue Bird* and was exposed to yet another new concept. If the dead weren't really dead as long as they lived in memory, then her father was alive, at least in her thoughts. She could bring him to life whenever she remembered him. The idea comforted her.

In July, she took the train from Lake Balaton to Dombovar, to stay with her cousin Evi Sas. Although she missed the lake, she fell into her familiar sisterly relationship with Evi. Hannah regretted keenly the fact that Evi had been rejected by Hannah's school. She had heard this news while she was at the lake and was so crushed with disappointment she fled the room and cried. If Evi had been taken by her school, they would have lived together most of the year. But it was not to be. Maybe this was an example of fate stepping in, directing their lives.

During this contemplative summer she wrote two poems. One she gave to her mother as a birthday present; the other she did not show anyone, but recorded in her diary:

17

Life is a brief and hurtling day,
Pain and striving fill every page.
Just time enough to glance around,
Register a face or sound
and — life's been around.

When school started again that fall, the pace quickened. She began piano lessons, continued tutoring, attended an international swimming match with George, saw the movie, *The Scarlet Pimpernel* after reading the book in English, wrote a play, and moved into a new house on Bimbó Street, only a few streets from their old place in Rose Hill.

There were other changes in Hannah's life. She became a vegetarian, then rejected it when the man who had designed his version of a meatless diet didn't respond to questions she asked him in a letter. Already Hannah refused to be spoon-fed other people's ideas. She raised thought-provoking issues and drew her own conclusions.

She also questioned the purpose of organized religion. On the second day of the Jewish New Year in 1936, she attended synagogue with her family, then confided in her diary:

I am not quite clear just how I stand; synagogue, religion, the question of God.

Around this time she toyed with possible careers. She considered going to Switzerland to learn hotel management. But she didn't take this idea very seriously. Hannah felt hotel management was too practical and dull for someone as creative as she was. She thought about being a teacher. Tutoring students was a rewarding experience, and she loved children. At Lake Balaton that summer, she had been closer to Judy's little sister than to Judy, her classmate.

She leaned toward professions that combined creativity along with her natural leadership qualities. One winter, while sick in bed with pleurisy, she had happily entertained herself by planning a children's summer camp at Lake Balaton. She wrote about this plan in her diary, even working out a typical day's schedule. But that dream was far off in the future, for when she was "about twenty."

More and more, though, Hannah was drawn to writing. She had been writing poetry since she was six. In school her compositions won prizes. After penning the "Brief and Hurtling Day" poem, she admitted in her diary that she would like to follow in her father's footsteps and be a writer, too. But she had not yet decided to make writing her career. At this time she looked upon writing as a way to please her father. He was gone, yet she believed he was still with her. She wanted her father to be proud of her. In her diary she wrote:

> I know I have a little talent, but I don't think it's more than that. Although the desire to write is constantly alive within me, I still don't consider writing my life's goal or ambition,

but rather a way of making myself and those around me happy.

But the following year, Hannah's attitude changed. She wrote a play and performed it for her family. Her play was a great success and she enjoyed basking in the glow of praise. Hannah's tentative longing crystalized into true ambition. She announced her new vocation in her diary, in June 1936:

I would like to be a writer. For the time I just laugh at myself; I've no idea whether I have any talent.

Later that summer she confessed that her desire to be a writer was even stronger. "It's my constant wish," she wrote. "And I would like to be a great soul," she added fervently. "If God will permit!"

The next day she scolded herself for writing such conceited notions. "Big Soul!" she wrote. "I'm just a struggling fifteen-year-old girl whose principal preoccupation is coping with herself."

Hannah was usually able to see herself with unclouded vision. But when it came to "the boy situation," her perception blurred.

Her brother George asked if she was interested in boys. "Well, yes, they interest me more than before," Hannah replied in her diary. It was not always easy to meet boys, however. She went to a girls' school and spent her summers in the company of Evi or girlfriends. But if she did see a boy, chances were he would not live up to her standards.

She listed these qualifications in her diary:

This is my idea of the ideal boy: he should be attractive and well-dressed, but not a fop; he should be a good sportsman, but interested in other things besides sports; he should be cultured and intelligent, but good-humored, and not arrogant; and he should not chase after girls. And so far I have not met a single boy like this.

By the time Hannah was fifteen, boys suddenly became interested in *her*. And she was confused. Boys were attracted to her intelligence and lively appetite for life, not necessarily her looks — the very traits Hannah herself found admirable. Yet she turned them away, unsure of her own feelings.

When one boy in particular, Gaby, pursued Hannah, she was flattered by his attention. In May, 1936, she wrote:

One of the boys said he couldn't understand what Gaby saw in me, whereupon George said I was very intelligent . . . Hearing this his friend said, "Well, that's something."

But a few weeks later, Hannah backed away from Gaby's pursuit. He came over to Hannah's house so they could do physics homework together. Suddenly Gaby scribbled *I love you* in her notebook. Flustered, Hannah closed the notebook. Later she took a cold view of the incident, writing in her diary:

> The Gaby affair continues: yesterday he "confessed" his love . . . I suppose it's my fate to have boys of my own age confessing their love in writing . . . I don't think I really like him much, except as a sort of chum.

Gaby was determined to win Hannah over. He lent her a book with a picture of himself tucked in the pages. The photo was autographed, *With Love Forever, Gaby*. Hannah didn't say a word about the unusual bookmark. Shortly afterward, he came over to her house. During a game of Ping-Pong, Gaby asked her to marry him.

Between volleys, Hannah calmly said she'd already had two proposals of marriage.

Humiliated, Gaby tried to embarrass her. How would she react if he asked her to marry him in ten years, he wanted to know.

Hannah terminated the discussion by pointing out that they were both only fifteen.

Almost angrily, she elaborated on the matter in her diary:

> When I began keeping a diary I decided I would write only about beautiful and serious things, and under no circumstances constantly about boys, as most girls do . . . Well, now my diary has become like that of any

fifteen-year-old girl, with nothing serious in it . . .

Despite her resolve not to go overboard about boys and clothes, Hannah was delighted with her first long dress. It was blue taffeta, a shade that complimented her eyes. She wore the gown to a concert.

Like any teenage girl, Hannah had disagreements with her mother. Ordinarily they got along fine, better than most mothers and daughters, drawn together by the loss of Bela Senesh. Hannah wrote, in a wounded tone, of one such flare-up:

I was reading something and Mama took it out of my hand, saying it was not a proper thing for me to read. This hurt me very much as it was a letter from school addressed to Mama, and I felt I could read it, too.

She still did not know about the matter of her school fees. Her mother wanted to protect her from unpleasantness. But she could not protect her for long.

"Horrible!" Hannah wrote earlier in October, 1935, about the war between Italy and Ethiopia. "Now there is nothing left to do but pray this war will remain a local one, and end as quickly as possible," she concluded.

A year later Hannah attended the funeral procession of the former Hungarian Prime Minister. She was rather bored with the event, remarking carelessly in her diary that she had liked the flowers. As for the famous people in the procession — including Nazi leader Hermann Goering, and Mussolini's son-in-law — Hannah wasn't the least bit impressed. She couldn't have known that Goering was the head of Hitler's new secret police, the Gestapo, or that Mussolini would soon join forces with Hitler and create a dangerous alliance. Storm clouds were brewing, but the storm had not yet broken.

Around this time, she read *War and Peace* by Leo Tolstoy. At first she plowed through the complicated plot eagerly, caught up in the history of the Napoleonic invasion of Russia in 1812. Toward the end her enthusiam flagged, but she doggedly finished the book. She commented on the author's message in her diary:

It is obvious he does not think the roles played by individuals in the enactment of history were nearly as important or decisive as one generally believes.

The rumbles of war grew louder. Two years after Hitler proclaimed the Third Reich, the Nuremberg Laws were passed. These laws deprived German Jews of their citizenship and their right to earn a living. Many of those Jews emigrated to a land in the Middle East then called Palestine, which was open to Jews. Hatred against the Jews was spreading rapidly, due to Hitler's propaganda. Feelings

24

of anti-Semitism spilled over into neighboring nations.

When Hannah went to Dombovar that summer to visit Evi, she saw ominous signals. The beach was now segregated. Jews were required to swim in one part, Christians in the other. Hannah wrote of these changes in her diary, discouraged because the rule meant little chance to meet boys:

There are a great many non-Jewish boys, but the segregation here is so sharply defined one can't possibly think of mixing, or imagine that a Christian boy would ever go near a Jewish girl. This segregation often seems comical, but actually it is a sad and disquieting sign.

The storm was fast approaching.

3
Leaving

Hannah began the new school term after an event-filled summer. She took a trip to Italy and then to Dombovar, where she celebrated her sixteenth birthday. Then she was interviewed as a "poetess." She pronounced the resulting newspaper article "quite good."

Elation was followed by despair. Fini Mama died. Catherine Senesh was grief-stricken. Hannah and Evi did most of the cooking, settled out-of-town relatives, and helped with funeral arrangements. Hannah capably shouldered part of her mother's burden.

The new term was only a few weeks old when Hannah confronted anti-Semitism head-on. The incident revolved around her position as an officer in the Literary Society. She had been nominated, along with other classmates, at an earlier meeting, and had won the election.

Being an officer was not new to her. The year before she had been treasurer of the Stenographic Circle and secretary of the Bible Society. Efficient and popular, Hannah was used to holding positions of authority in various clubs and groups. Because of her writing interest, she most enjoyed her membership in the Literary Society.

The previous term, she had attended meetings with her friend Agi, who was also a writer. Both girls read their poems to the group, which consisted mainly of older girls. In February, 1937, Hannah wrote in her diary:

I just got back from the Literary Society, where I read "The Ice Cream Man," which the Society considered good. But I thought Agi's two poems were much better . . . Now I constantly wonder whether my poems are as good as Agi's. Goodness, it would be wonderful to be truly talented.

In May of that same term, elections were discussed. The teacher reminded the group that girls nominated to the posts had to be Protestant. Hannah, hoping she might be elected to one of the coveted offices, felt depressed at the news. "Should I put myself out and work for the improvement of the Society's standards," she wrote in her diary, "even though I am now aware of the spirit that motivates it, or should I drop the whole thing?"

She *was* elected and attended the first meeting, ready to perform the duties of her office. She was the only 7th Form student on the board. The Literary Society was run by 8th Form girls, though one office was traditionally held by a 7th Form girl.

But at the meeting, the 8th Form leaders called for a new election, stating the rule that a Jewish girl could not hold office. Hannah's classmates voiced their objections. The Society was supposed to accept officers elected by the class.

Not this time. The President asked for new nominations. Two girls were nominated quickly to run against Hannah. Votes were taken and counted. Hannah sat through the proceedings, knowing what the outcome would be. When one of her friends, a Gentile, was elected, she told Hannah she did not deserve the post.

As Hannah later reported to her mother, she advised her friend to accept the job. It mattered little who most deserved the job, only that the person was not a Jew. Hannah brushed the incident off as class politics. But in her diary, she confided her hurt:

Now I don't want to take part in, or have anything to do with the work of the Society, and don't care about it any more.

Although Hannah earned top marks in school again this year, her enthusiasm had vanished.

"Life at school is rather dull," she wrote. Boys were still attracted to her. She went out with a few different boys off and on, but they didn't really interest her. She didn't write in her diary for weeks at a time. When she did, the brief entries were about trivial events.

And then on March 13, 1938, the day after Hitler occupied Austria, Hannah recorded the tension that reverberated throughout Budapest. "In school, on the street, even at parties, it is the main topic of discussion," she wrote of Austria's surrender to the Nazis. Hungarians had every cause to be nervous — Austria bordered their homeland.

During spring vacation, she went to visit Evi. On the train to Dombovar, a young man sat next to her. Sensing he wanted to strike up an acquaintance, she got out the book she was reading, *The Moon and Sixpence,* hoping to discourage conversation. Undeterred, the young man asked her if he could smoke, if she was going to Dombovar, and so forth. The chatty young man, a Presbyterian student, told her she ought to take divinity classes. She replied that that would be impossible, certain that he would take the hint and leave her alone, but he then demanded she tell him her name. When she did not answer, the rude young man huffily asserted that Jews typically refused to mix with other people.

This unsettling incident was added to the disasterous Literary Society meeting. Hannah carried both inside, confused by the events taking place around her.

The rumblings grew menacingly close. The First Jewish Bill, debated hotly by the Hungarian Congress and passed in May, 1938, was designed to limit Jewish participation in business to twenty percent of the total number of people in each profession. The bill, passed as law, further implied that letting Jews get ahead financially was dangerous to the nation. "I wonder how this will end?" Hannah asked her diary.

The Senesh family was directly affected by these disturbing changes when George graduated that spring. He had intended to continue his studies in Austria, but now he had to switch his plans to France. At the graduation ceremony, Hannah noticed a few of George's classmates wore the uniform of the Arrow Cross, a Hungarian fascist party similar to the Nazis. Her brother approached the boys and asked them to look after his mother and sister while he was gone. The boys just stared at him. *Look after Jews?* their expressions seemed to say.

On the last day of her own term, Hannah collected the second prize she had won in a photography competition. Photography was the only activity she had participated in that year. Sticking to her vow, she had not gone to the Literary Society since the day she was shunned by the older girls.

Her diary was full. In it, she had recorded her hopes and fears, her triumphs . . . and her disappointments. She immediately began another diary in a new composition book, sensing that she would have more to write about with each passing day as the world shifted under her feet.

After school it was off to Lake Balaton again, this time to the town of Lelle with another school friend, Lisbeth.

George's train passed through Lelle. Hannah arranged to meet him at the station. He was on his way to Lyons, where he was going to study textiles.

Their last conversation consisted of trivial matters, like tennis rackets and suntans. Hannah chattered away until the train started moving. Back in her room, she let her true feelings tumble out. George was leaving for France — another member of their small family going away. She wrote a poem, entitled "Farewell," expressing her feelings.

Hannah's seventeenth summer sped by. She had her palm read by a gypsy, who predicted that she would be a bride within a year, her husband would own a car, they would not be rich but happy, and they would have one son! She and Evi went to the mountains for three weeks and shared early sunrises, picked dew-fresh strawberries, and hunted four-leaf clovers. Hannah also received another marriage proposal, this time from a boy named Danny who claimed he had been in love with her for years and demanded an answer "yes or no." Of course she turned him down, but wondered if the fortune-teller's prediction was rubbish after all. Was this another instance of destiny stepping in?

As for her writing, she was not about to leave her future career to chance. Taking matters into her own hands, she requested an interview with

Piroska Reichardt, the editor of a well-respected literary magazine. She needed a professional opinion. Was her work any good? Reichardt read Hannah's poems and declared them "better than average," though somewhat long and lacking in form. Then she told Hannah that she did have talent and would become a writer. Hannah left the meeting elated. "Somehow, one has more confidence after professional criticism," she wrote in her diary.

When school began that fall, summer pleasures faded rapidly. Hannah was apprehensive about school, afraid the previous year's Literary Society would hang over her. As tensions mounted, there was talk of war. On September 30, 1938, the Munich Agreement was signed, surrendering part of Czechoslovakia called the Sudetenland to Germany. Most people breathed a little easier, thinking Hitler's greedy appetite had been satisfied.

Yet Jews were still understandably nervous. Hannah attended a party at her friend Mary's house. Mary's family had recently converted to Christianity, since it was no longer desirable to be a Jew. Hannah could not condone such an act. "Only now am I beginning to see what it really means to be a Jew in a Christian society," she wrote earlier in her diary. ". . . you have to be someone exceptional to fight anti-Semitism, which is the most difficult kind of fight." Renouncing one's religious beliefs was the coward's way out.

In Hungary the situation worsened when Regent

Horthy appointed a new Prime Minister, Count Teleki. Believing Jews were a threat to the country, Teleki vigorously promoted the Second Jewish Bill. The second bill restricted Jews from holding government offices, obtaining business licenses, buying land, and working as judges, lawyers, writers, or teachers.

Pressured by war news and escalating feelings of anti-Semitism, Hannah decided she had to take a stand, one way or the other.

She became a Zionist.

The Zionist movement was not new. For centuries, ever since the Roman conquest of Jerusalem in 63 B.C., Jews had wanted to reclaim their Homeland. After they were driven out of what was later called Palestine, these scattered, or dispersed, Jews were forced to live in other countries. In response to European anti-Semitism late in the nineteenth century, the Zionist movement was born. The Jews would return to Palestine and form a Jewish nation.

Hannah wholeheartedly embraced Zionist principles. She wrote passionately in her diary:

> . . . I now consciously and strongly feel that I am a Jew, and am proud of it. My primary aim is to go to Palestine, to work for it.

Zionism appealed to Hannah's idealistic tendencies. She joined the Maccabee Society, a local Zionist organization, and took lessons in Hebrew, the language spoken by Jews in Palestine. Her commitment to Zionism overshadowed everything else in her life. She lost interest in school and no longer wanted to have fun with her friends. None of those things mattered any more. She had a new goal and she pursued it with singleminded determination. She was going to Palestine as soon as she graduated.

Her mother, however, was less enthusiastic over Hannah's decision. With her son in Paris during uncertain times, Catherine Senesh did not want to lose her daughter, too.

Mrs. Senesh wrote of their disagreements in an account of Hannah's childhood. She told Hannah she could not become a writer if she emigrated, implying that although Hannah might speak Hebrew, she would think in Hungarian. What about her desire to be a writer?

Hannah briskly dismissed this argument. "That question is dwarfed by present burning problems."

Eventually Hannah wore her mother down. Catherine Senesh reluctantly gave her permission.

Hannah was already making preparations. In March, 1939, she wrote to the Agricultural School in Nahalal for admission information. This action spurred another argument with her mother.

Mrs. Senesh protested that Hannah would be wasting her talents in the fields. Why didn't she apply to the University instead?

Hannah, of course, had a ready answer. "There are already too many intellectuals in Palestine; the need is for workers who can help build the country. Who can do the work if not we, the youth?"

During spring break, Hannah and her mother went to Lyons to visit George. When she saw her brother, she told him she had become a Zionist and was going to Palestine. To her delight, George exclaimed he was a Zionist, too. They made plans to meet in Palestine, after George completed his studies. Mrs. Senesh sat quietly, unable to participate in their discussion, though her children tried to convince her to come with them. Hannah could not understand why her mother wanted to stay in Budapest, but Catherine Senesh did not want to leave her home.

Hannah, however, no longer felt Budapest was *her* home. Hungary had abandoned her, along with the other Jews. If only her mother could see that.

In July Hannah passed her final exams. She graduated *summa cum laude*, with the highest honors. Her teachers tried to persuade her to stay and go to the University. With her grades, they said, she should have little trouble getting in, meaning that most Jews were restricted. Hannah was not tempted by the offer. She did not want to be a student with no future; she wanted to make a real difference in the world. She could not do that in Hungary.

As soon as school was out, she left for Dombovar. She began writing her diary in Hebrew, for practice. Her spirit was already in Palestine — now if she could just get the rest of herself there!

Hannah worked outside in her aunt's garden,

pulling weeds in the hot sun to accustom herself to the climate of Palestine.

A few days after her eighteenth birthday, her immigration certificate came in the mail. "I've got it! I've got it!" Hannah wrote jubilantly in her diary. She had to be in Palestine by the end of September. Her next problem was transportation.

It was not easy to leave Hungary. Borders were closing every day as the storm grew closer. Hannah hounded travel agencies, representatives to Palestine, and the Jewish Social Aid office, trying to obtain passage tickets and the necessary travel documents. She worried so much, she made herself sick.

One morning in August she woke with a pain around her heart. Terrified she had contracted the same illness that had claimed her father's life, she went to a doctor, who diagnosed her problem as nervous tension.

On September 1, 1939, Germany invaded Poland. Two days later, Britain declared war on Germany, in defense of its Polish ally. France followed Britain's lead.

The storm clouds broke. World War II had started.

Now travel agencies were choked with Jews and other people anxious to put distance between themselves and the war zone. Hannah was afraid she wouldn't get out before her deadline was up.

At last an official who had known Hannah's father arranged her exit visa. He rushed the papers through. Hannah linked herself with a group of

Slovaks bound for Palestine, booking passage on the train and steamship. They were leaving the next day.

"I felt as though ice were flowing through my veins," Catherine Senesh wrote later. The moment she had been dreading for months had arrived. Her daughter was leaving.

All that night Hannah and her mother packed Hannah's things. Grandmother Senesh and other relatives and close friends came to say goodbye.

Departure day finally dawned. It was September 13, 1939, less than two weeks after war had been declared.

When the time came to walk out the door, Hannah paused. Both she and her mother tried not to cry. As Catherine Senesh later wrote, Hannah threw herself in the housekeeper's arms, crying, "Rosi, take care of Mama."

Then she climbed in beside her mother and the cab pulled away from the house on Bimbó Street.

DISTANT LIGHTS
1939–1943

4
A New Beginning

Hannah Senesh's train was scheduled to depart in the afternoon. Her taxi delivered her to the huge glass-and-iron depot of the Oriental Station. The station echoed with the noise of passengers and clattering baggage carts. One of Senesh's aunts took charge of customs and her luggage. All too soon it was time to board the train.

Senesh had managed to bottle up her emotions until then but (as her mother later wrote) she nearly broke down as she looked out the window at her mother standing on the platform.

It was Rosh Hashanah, the Jewish New Year. Catherine Senesh would be going home to an empty house and would perform the ritual of lighting the candles alone. In an account of her daughter's childhood, Mrs. Senesh reflected on that September afternoon:

The tensions of the last weeks, the excitement, were overshadowed by the parting, the final break, and the total uncertainty of the future. As the train inched out, a great cloud seemed to fall over the entire station.

After a few hours of staring at the Hungarian countryside, Senesh hauled her new portable typewriter onto her lap and began a letter. She had to let her mother know how torn she felt about leaving. She was anxious to make a place for herself in Palestine, but felt great sorrow in parting from the person she loved most in the world. Her letter concluded:

. . . my thoughts are constantly with you, and I shall spend this New Year holiday with you in spirit. Don't be upset, Mother, that this letter is so empty. When one has a great deal to say one can't find words — beyond these two: dearest Mother.

She wrote again to her mother four days later, on board the steamship *Bessarabia*. If she felt homesick, she did not give a clue in her letter, in which she chattered brightly about shipboard life and her accommodations, an upper berth by a porthole. One of her cabin mates was from Palestine, so she was able to practice her Hebrew. She also spoke Hebrew to the Jewish children born in Palestine, who were returning home after visiting relatives. Jews born in Palestine are called *sabras*.

Sunrises at sea tempted the poet in Senesh. She had risen at six that morning and gone to the top deck to watch the sun come up.

Later that day their ship docked at Istanbul. Once again Senesh was topside, lounging in a deck chair, her typewriter on her knees. Passengers weren't allowed to disembark at the port, so she had to make do with the view from the rail. She described the skyline of the mosques and minarets in her letter to her mother.

On September 21, the *Bessarabia* glided into the calm waters of the port of Haifa. After seven days of travel — two on the train, five aboard ship — Hannah Senesh had finally arrived in Palestine.

Haifa wasn't at all what she expected. From her reading of the early Jewish pioneers of Palestine, she knew the people who preceded her had struggled to build a home in the harsh land. These pioneers were called *Halutzim* after the ancient language of Hebrew was revived as their new native tongue. The first wave of settlers drained swamps and established colonies, but were mainly unprepared for the difficulties. Many of those earlier settlers died of malaria. Others abandoned the cause and left Palestine. The second group of pioneers, many fleeing Russian persecution around the turn of the century, was more determined to succeed. They realized that in order to survive in the desert, they would have to live together, share property, and work for the good of the group, rather than the individual. The communities they formed were called *kibbutzim*.

Senesh was amazed to see that Haifa, the main port city of Palestine, was not a wilderness of camps and camels. The city spread before her was quite modern, with endless docks, oil refineries, and new housing developments clambering up Mount Carmel. The older part of the city coexisted neatly with the new section.

When Senesh disembarked, she was immediately engulfed by crowds of people from many different cultures and nationalities — Arabs, Jews, Europeans. The sun was very bright, yet the air was crisp and dry.

Her poet's eye delighted in the colorful display at a dockside market: black olives, oranges, eggplants, artichokes, raisins, and garlic. Market people hawked their wares in Hebrew and Hebrew signs advertised stores and buses. Here Jews were not restricted, not treated as undesirable foreigners. Here they could breathe clean air, walk freely.

She was home.

A Zionist organization official met Senesh and helped her retrieve her baggage. He then deposited her at the doorstep of the Krausz family, where she was staying a few days, giving her time to get a typhus vaccination and explore the city.

Perceptive as always, she noticed the difference between Palestinian Jews and Hungarian Jews.

The Palestinian Jews looked as if they worked hard, but were working for themselves. To Senesh they appeared to be more alive.

After two days in Haifa, she boarded the Egged Company bus for the final leg of her journey, the Agricultural School in Nahalal, less than a half hour away.

The bus jounced through the desert. Senesh saw cactus for the first time. They drove past Arab villages of crude wooden houses — a sharp contrast to the modern Jewish settlements — flocks of sheep and goats, endless windblown brush.

Nahalal overlooked the valley of Jezreel, which was now called the Emek. Originally a swamp, the Emek was a patchwork of orchards and well-tended fields. Senesh was inspired by the achievements of those who had come to Palestine less than thirty-five years before. Those halutzim had battled disease and blazing heat. Many gave their lives to help shape the Land. Now that she had a firsthand glimpse of the results of their labor, she was eager to work the soil herself, become a part of this nation.

"I know I still see things idealistically," she wrote to her mother, "and I know there will be difficult days ahead."

The village of Nahalal was a collective farming settlement, or *moshav*. In a moshav each family owned property, livestock, and their house. This type of settlement differed from the kibbutz, where property and work were shared by its members.

Nahalal was founded the same summer Hannah Senesh was born, 1921, and was a planned community from the start. Houses surrounded an oval of public buildings. Private garden plots connected the public grounds to each individual's house, like the spokes of a wheel. Surrounding the Agricultural School, acres of emerald-green fields and orchards grew with a lushness that defied the arid climate.

Then came the three dormitory buildings of the school. The first building, Senesh learned, was for new students, and that was where she was assigned. The facility was small, but comfortable. There were approximately 150 girls in the school, compared to the nearly 1,000 students at her old high school in Budapest. For the first time in her life, she would share a room.

Senesh had two roommates. Pnina was originally from Poland, but had been in *Eretz Israel* some time. People who were from Palestine or who had lived there a good while called it Eretz Israel which meant the Land of Israel, or simply Eretz, the Land. Hannah's other roommate was Miriam. Two years older than Senesh, she had just arrived in Palestine from Bulgaria. The girls, wearing slacks and kerchiefs, were on their way to the fields.

Hannah Senesh began to unpack. It was September 22, 1939, Yom Kippur Eve. For the first time, she would not attend the service with her mother. Suddenly she felt a tidal wave of homesickness. "I made an accounting of what I had left behind, and what I had found here, and I didn't know know whether the move would prove worthwhile," she wrote the next day. She gave in to her homesickness and cried.

5
Taking Root

Within a few weeks, Hannah Senesh had adjusted to the new routine. She even looked like a Palestinian, with the requisite headscarf, sunglasses, and pants she wore to work in the fields. She learned to cream her face to protect her skin. Even though it was now mid-October, the sun was high and powerful in the daytime, life-draining. Warm winds blew constantly, twisting the scrubby desert brush and making one's skin as tough as leather. The women and girls in the village had the nut-brown skin of dried apples.

When Senesh first arrived, she picked olives, "easy but monotonous work," she wrote her mother. Climbing trees was fun, but it took a great many olives to fill a bucket. Then she was assigned to fertilize the vineyards. While her letters home were chatty and cheerful, Senesh confessed her true feelings in letters to George: ". . . this kind of work is not as simple as I thought. One needs knowledge of the craft. . . ."

Senesh lacked the skills to do the most basic chores. She had been brought up gently, and knew nothing of ironing or scrubbing floors, much less fertilizing vineyards. Domestic chores had always been performed by Rosika. Hannah Senesh had never even had to make her bed. But her desire to become a useful member of the Land spurred her to overcome her deficiencies. What she didn't know, she learned.

Her old determination, which had briefly deserted her the first day in Nahalal, returned in full force. She did not give in to tears again. When asked if she was homesick, she replied truthfully that she was not. "The atmosphere of home . . . I really don't miss," she wrote in her diary. "But I do miss Mother and George very much."

In a letter home to her mother, Senesh described one typical day. It began at 5:30, with the first bell. She and her roommates dressed and stripped their beds, then went to their first class of the day. The girls studied subjects that related to agriculture and farming: chemistry, botany, general agriculture, fruit gardening, dairy farming. The small classes were divided into two groups, depending on the student's knowledge of Hebrew. Senesh was in the A class for advanced students. She was thankful she had had the foresight to learn Hebrew before she came.

At this school, teachers were more relaxed and

let the girls call them by their first names. Senesh was surprised she did not have to rise to her feet when asked a question by the teacher, but she soon accepted the informal attitude.

Their first class lasted from six to seven. Then the girls hurried to breakfast. The food was also very different from what Senesh had been used to in Hungary, lighter, but still filling. That morning she devoured a grilled tomato half, a wedge of cheese, bread and butter, and tea. They could have as much of anything as they wished, except for sugar for their tea, which was rationed to one lump per girl.

After breakfast the girls returned to their rooms and made their beds. This week it was again Senesh's turn to clean the room. She swept the floor, dusted, picked up clothes and books and shoes, then scrubbed the stone floor.

Chores finished, Senesh reported for her first work detail by eight o'clock. She worked steadily, shoveling manure around the base of the grapevines. Her arms were tired, but at least she'd learned to pace herself so her back did not hurt.

Shortly before noon, the girls started checking the position of the sun in the heat-whitened sky. Senesh was hungry, too. She had about three minutes to wash and pull a comb through her hair.

In the dining hall Senesh sat down at a table with nine other girls. She looked at the food on her plate wondering what it was, but too polite to ask. Boiled eggs in a cold tomato sauce? She took a bite — whatever its name, the dish was delicious.

She cleaned her plate, then drank the chilled grapefriuit juice that was dessert. She was very thirsty. They weren't allowed to have water with their meal. After lunch, when they had cooled off, they could drink all the water they wanted.

The girls had an hour's rest before they began their afternoon work. Senesh went back to her room, washed her hair, and sat outside in the sun to dry it. It felt good just to *sit*.

At 1:30, she resumed hcr work in the vineyard. The afternoon passed more quickly than the morning. At three o'clock, she raced into the dining hall. She had learned the hard way that to be even a minutc late for tea meant no jam on her bread.

After tea, she took a much-needed shower and changed her clothes. They had two free hours. Miriam had set up the ironing board and was ironing blouses. Hannah added ironing and laundering to her list of newly-acquired skills. She summed up her feelings about working in the laundry in her diary: "I must admit it has little educational value."

At the end of the two hours, she went to the last class of the day with Miriam and Pnina. Pnina was still a bit distant, but Miriam was turning out to be a good friend. When they were alone, Senesh confided her hopes and dreams of making a real contribution to the Land.

When the class was over at 7:30, the girls went to supper. By this time Hannah was feeling pretty tired, and after supper she and her roommates went back to their room. Pnina usually switched on the radio so they could listen to the news. Hannah was keenly interested in what was happening in France and Hungary. She hoped George would be able to leave France and come to Palestine soon. And she worried about her mother.

In the evenings, when the workday was behind her and the night drifted across the Valley, Hannah often reread her mother's letters. Her mother had written that Evi was staying in Budapest. Hannah was glad; her mother wouldn't be so completely alone now. She wrote long letters home, detailing her work and classes. She included Evi in the greeting, knowing her mother would share the letter, and sent extra kisses to George, hoping the letter would then be forwarded to Lyons. Her diary went neglected for weeks. She was too tired and too busy to keep up regular entries. Letters home would have to do for now.

The girls studied and played the radio softly. Hannah Senesh finished her letter before lights out, at 9:30.

Fall dissolved into winter. December and January in Palestine were nothing like those snowbound months in Hungary. Here the nights got cooler, but the days were pleasant, more like spring. Senesh was working in the dairy. Swathed in a rubber apron over her trousers and boots, she washed the huge cows, amazing herself that she wasn't the least bit afraid of them. She made the beasts behave by swearing at them in Hungarian because she didn't know how to swear in Hebrew, she confessed in a letter to her mother. She embellished the letter with funny sketches of herself falling into a manure pile.

By now she was used to hard work and was able to laugh at herself. She enjoyed her studies. She got along with all the girls. She managed the same balancing act she performed in Budapest — doing well in school without sacrificing popularity. This was one of her most enduring traits, the ability to master any task set before her while maintaining the trust and friendship of those around her.

Life wasn't all work and studies. She had fun, too. On Friday evenings, the girls sang and played music. Saturdays, they played Ping-Pong or held dances. Boys dropped by from the village. As her Hebrew improved, Senesh began to feel at home in the Land she had chosen.

This feeling intensified when she had the chance to see the country. During the Hanukkah holidays, she visited Haifa, which she had only glimpsed upon her arrival four months earlier. She stayed with the Krausz family again and attended parties, wearing the dresses that had hung uselessly in her cupboard. But she found the city didn't tempt her, and she was content to return to Nahalal.

Her next trip wasn't until April of 1940. This time she and a couple of girls from school hitched a ride to Tiberias. Her mother would have been shocked if she had seen her daughter waving at cars from the middle of the road. Hitchhiking was an acceptable method of transportation in Palestine, as few people had cars.

They caught a ride with an Englishman and

drove past places like Nazareth and the Sea of Galilee that brought the Bible to life. The Englishman dropped the girls off. They picnicked by the water, feasting on fresh fruit and ice cream, then wandered around the Arab quarter. Soon it was time to go back. On the road to Nahalal, Senesh's classmates paced, worried that they wouldn't get another ride. Senesh perched on a mailbox in the shade and sang, unconcerned.

When a car appeared, her friends flagged it wildly. The man braked, thinking there were only two girls, then suddenly Senesh jumped down from the mailbox and hurled herself into the car. The driver slammed the door, afraid more savages would pile into his car, but she assured him that only three little girls needed a ride. In Budapest, she never would have behaved so boldly, but here the rules were different. Senesh was learning to adapt.

At the end of the term, as soon as exams were over, she and Miriam took their first real holiday. For two weeks, they thumbed rides and stayed overnight in *kibbutzim*, to keep costs down. They travelled around the Sea of Galilee and up the rocky border of northern Palestine. After staying the night in Kfar Giladi, Hannah got up early the next morning to climb the foothills of the nearby mountains, called the Heights of Naftali. She brought her diary along on the trip, hoping to record each new impression. On the mountaintop, she stood with her arms reaching toward the bright blue sky. High up in the thin, clean air, she felt closer to God. Here her thoughts became lofty, too, and she wondered if she would be able to serve, if God called upon her.

They visited other settlements, where workers had just begun to carve out a community in the forbidding countryside. She was able to see the end result of her training. When she graduated from Nahalal Agricultural School, she would be qualified to help build the land she had grown to love.

She returned to school with renewed enthusiasm. More than ever she believed she had made the right decision.

Of course there were times when she experienced a twinge of homesickness. In February, Evi sent her a postcard, describing a party she had gone to. Hannah turned the postcard over, noting her torn nails and work-roughened hands. She looked like a laborer, she realized.

She was not really envious of Evi's social life. She could have stayed in Hungary and had a glamorous social life, but she didn't need that. She belonged to the Land.

In a letter to her mother, Hannah wanted her mother to know that the sacrifice she had made allowing her only daughter to emigrate to a faraway land was worth the pain of separation.

"It was worth coming for the sensation of feeling that I am the equal of all men in my own country," she wrote.

Hannah Senesh had become her own person.

6
Difficult Days

By September, 1940, her first anniversary in Palestine, Senesh had settled into her new life. The other girls looked upon her as both a good friend and a leader. A firm believer in democracy, Senesh felt decisions should be made by the members of the community, not one person.

But she also liked to make decisions on her own. In a letter home she admitted, "My work is pleasant now inasmuch as I work entirely independently. I do what I think best when I think best to do it. . . ." She had a way of quietly defying authority and backing her acts of defiance with sound reasoning. She was rarely chastised. Not yet twenty, Senesh was learning that the boundaries of authority were not set in concrete.

But for now it was enough to be a student. She saw her two years at Nahalal Agricultural School as a stepping-stone. Training would allow her to become a capable worker. Her goal — first, last, and always — was to help build Palestine into a homeland for Jews

To that end, she worked in the school kitchen and laundry. She learned to bake bread in big batches, using 130 pounds of flour, and kneading the dough by hand. She scoured the stalls and feed troughs in the milking shed. Her Hebrew improved, though she wondered if she would ever write poetry in that language. She read the poems of Rachel, an early settler who wrote honestly about the hard work involved in creating a new country.

Gradually she became accustomed to the heat and began to appreciate the landscape, the browns and blues of earth meeting sky, the fields of wheat blowing in the hot dry wind, the still-startling sight of green plants advancing into the arid desert.

She was glad her first year of schooling was behind her. The second year promised to be more exciting — fewer housekeeping chores and more work in the fields. Already she was thinking about what branch of agriculture she would specialize in when she graduated. She was very good with chickens — perhaps she should be a poultry farmer. Or better yet, a poultry expert. She pictured herself traveling all over Palestine, demonstrating her poultry-raising skills. After visiting a nearby kibbutz, where she met the children of the workers, Senesh thought about being a teacher again. Here she could be anything she wanted, with no restrictions because of her religion.

Her new life would have been wonderful, except for two things: the war, and her loneliness.

At first, the faraway events of the war made Senesh feel she was on another planet. Students listened to reports on the radio every evening. The girls from Poland and Germany and Czechoslovakia were silent during the broadcasts, their thoughts undoubtedly with the families they had left behind.

Once Senesh found herself reading a page in her agricultural book over and over. Then she realized why the sentences were meaningless. Here she was, studying for an exam while war raged in Europe. Germany's power increased with each passing day. She felt ashamed reading about agriculture while thousands died.

She worried about her mother and George. Earlier that spring the world held its breath as German forces marched toward Paris. "Perhaps today the city will fall," Hannah Senesh wrote in her diary in June. It did, and her link to her brother was abruptly cut off.

From the relative safety of Nahalal, Senesh began to feel guilty. Her brother was trapped in a Nazi-occupied country. Her mother was alone in Hungary. "It's all my fault," Senesh confided regretfully to her diary. In her misery, she heaped blame upon herself.

I can't feel a thousandth part of what Mother must be living through. She is suffering for our plans, dreams, which perhaps in this world holocaust will turn to ashes . . . I can imagine her spending sleepless nights . . . And I, thousands of miles away, cannot sit beside her . . . calm her, share her worries.

When she heard radio reports about bombing raids over England, she couldn't believe thousands were dead. How could such things happen in a world where the skies were so blue, the land so green and peaceful?

But such things *were* happening. France, Poland, Denmark, the Netherlands, Czechoslovakia, Norway, Belgium — the roll call of countries Hitler now occupied lengthened. In the face of such wholesale destruction, Senesh began to wonder if her work was so important. Shortly after the invasion of France, she was gathering hay. The scent of the new-mown hay, coupled with the perfectness of the day, made her feel at one with the universe. Her steadfast belief in her goals, which had faltered with the terrible war news, was again reinforced. Even though she felt selfish coming to Palestine at such a time, she knew she would have been miserable in Hungary. "Each of us must find his own way . . . even though the entire world is on fire . . ." she wrote in her diary.

But a crack had appeared in Hannah Senesh's seemingly unshakable foundation. Once she questioned her decision to emigrate, she opened the door to other anxieties.

The war crept closer. Haifa, less than a half

hour's drive from Nahalal, was bombed four times that summer. Nahalal participated in the night-time blackouts. The girls drew heavy black curtains to hide lights that might attract German bombers. When Haifa was under attack, the girls were rushed to a shelter.

As Senesh began her second year at the school, she acutely felt the distance between Nahalal and Lyon. "It's been two years since I last saw my brother . . ." she wrote in her diary, "and I'm so afraid that by the time we meet again we'll be like strangers."

She was feeling like a stranger herself these days. She could talk to Miriam and confide in her diary, but that wasn't enough. "I need people," she wrote in April, 1940. "It's not even 'people' I need, but just *one* person." She longed to be in love.

In Palestine, as in Hungary, Senesh did not lack for admirers. She received not one but two marriage proposals by mail shortly after arriving in Nahalal. She wrote refusals to each boy, amused because their letters sounded so serious. What did boys that age know of love?

Boys from the village visited her from time to time and she met the brothers of fellow students. At first she was happy to stroll around the settlements and chat about trivial matters, but no one interested her. Now walking around with a boy just to pass the time pleasantly seemed like a waste of time. She didn't want casual acquaintances; she wanted love.

"I would love to have someone who loved me,"

she wrote in her diary in the spring of 1940, "and I would like to really love someone . . . I need a real love affair — or nothing."

And then she met Alex. He was funny and thoughtful and tried hard to please her. She wanted him to be the one.

They saw each other for nearly a year. Hannah wondered if she would find another boy as decent, honest, and kind as Alex. He truly loved her. She wasn't sure she loved *him* and dodged the question until the day Alex asked her to marry him. She could no longer avoid the issue. She and Alex came from different backgrounds, which did not bother her much. But Alex's goals for the future were very different from hers. *This* bothered her.

Alex wanted to work on a kibbutz, get married, raise children. Senesh wanted these things, too, but she wanted more. Living on a kibbutz would be fine for a year or two. She couldn't see herself doing that kind of work her whole life. Alex was ready to settle for an ordinary life. Unwilling to give up her dreams, she turned down his offer of marriage.

The decision left her unsettled. Not because she had refused to marry Alex — she knew she had done the right thing — but because she had let their relationship develop. She felt she had led him on.

She analyzed the breakup in her diary:

Naturally, it's difficult not to be impressed and

flattered by the love of a man of character, a man you respect and esteem. But this is still not love, and thus there is no reason to continue.

On her trip with Miriam earlier that summer, Hannah spent a happy day with a fisherman named Moshe. He wanted to write her, but she saw no point in corresponding because they had nothing in common. When Moshe asked to kiss her, Hannah backed away. In her diary she admitted she was too stiff around boys.

I thought about him after he left and realized I had actually been rather foolish . . . What harm would there have been in a kiss? Yet I could not . . . I suppose it's ridiculous that I'm still "waiting for the right one . . ."

Yet while she waited for the "right one" to come into her life and sweep her off her feet, she remained lonely.

Other fine, hairline cracks appeared. Outwardly Senesh was as efficient and dynamic as ever. She continued to work in the chicken house and orchards, take classes, participate in the Bible Society, and read Hebrew literature. But the physical work she had so craved back in Hungary began to lose its appeal. As she confided in a letter to her brother:

When I hoe, or clean something, or wash

dishes, or scatter the manure, I must confess the thought strikes me at times that I could be doing something better.

Ordinary tasks, those that had to be repeated daily, were rather boring. She added variety to the routine by inventing new procedures and short-cuts. In the spring of 1941, she toyed with a new method of checking eggs in the automatic brooder. But even that idea wore thin and Senesh chafed with impatience over endless chores and studies. Her impatience showed in her diary:

I've noticed at times I have the ability to in-fluence people . . . or to inspire them. Have I the right to waste this facility, hide it, ignore it, and to think about the automatic brooder instead?

She worried about wasting her talents. "I won-der," she wrote, "is this way I've chosen the right one?" Should she be more concerned with how to fill sacks of potatoes or solving problems of man-kind? "What binds me here?" she asked her diary. "My plans, my goal, all that which I have built within me this last year. Sometimes I feel it's a very shaky building . . ."

As the situation in Europe worsened, the cracks in her foundation widened.

"There are so many things I don't understand, least of all myself," Hannah Senesh wrote earlier. "I would like to know who I am . . . Either I have changed a lot, or the world around me has changed."

One evening she took a walk around Nahalal, too restless to study or write letters. Stars glittered overhead, so near. Lights from the houses lining the lane, mirrored the lights above. Snatches of radio music, singing, and people laughing and talking wafted out into the night. Dogs barked far-off warnings.

Senesh stopped, caught between the lights above and the lights around her. Her loneliness had never seemed so great as it did at that moment. She felt she was at a crossroads. The course of her life would be determined right there.

Should she head for the lights in the houses, be a part of that warm, laughing, singing world? Or should she aim for the stars, where the light was cold but burned so bright? Senesh knew she didn't fit into the ordinary world of houses and people, though she would certainly be happier there. No, she was destined for the stars . . . and loneliness.

When she got back to her room, she put her troubled thoughts in her diary:

What must I choose? The weak lights, filtering through the chinks in the houses, or the distant lights of stars? . . . Sometimes I feel I am an emissary who has been entrusted with a mission. What this mission is — is not clear to me . . . and why particularly me?

She could not settle for an ordinary life. Fate

had something more important in store for her. She would just have to wait to see what it was.

In April, 1941, Yugoslavia fell. By June, Greece and Crete knuckled under to Hitler and the fighting was fierce in Egypt and Syria. ". . . the war is virtually on our doorstep," Senesh wrote. Tel Aviv and Haifa were attacked. She and the others could here the booming explosions, which sounded like powerful fireworks.

In July she received a telegram from her mother. She could tell Catherine Senesh was afraid for her, now that Palestine was being drawn into the war. She did not want her mother to worry — things were bad enough in Hungary. She felt guilty that her life was safe and comfortable, while others were being killed and injured every day. ". . . I ought to do something . . . to justify my existence," she wrote, frustrated.

But what could she do? Would she fight if it came to that? She answered that question in a poem.

To die . . . so young to die . . . no, no, not I.
I love the warm sunny skies,
Light, songs, shining eyes.
I want no war, no battle cry —
No, no . . . Not I.
But if it must be that I live today
With blood and death on every hand,
Praised be He for the grace, I'll say
To live, if I should die this day . . .
Upon your soil, my home, my land.

At the end of July, 1941, Senesh turned in her final assignments. She scored 9's and 10's, the highest marks one could earn. School was nearly over.

She turned twenty that summer. She viewed the first twenty years of her life as a closed chapter. She was through preparing for life. Now she could begin fulfilling her destiny.

She was ready to set out for those distant lights.

7
The Kibbutz by the Sea

"**T**oday I washed 150 pairs of socks," Hannah Senesh wrote in her diary, February 9, 1942. "I thought I'd go mad. No, that's not really true. I didn't think of anything."

She washed the socks in a tub of seawater, then strung them on lines stretched between the tents and wooden huts of the Kibbutz Sdot-Yam. The wind blowing off the sea was cold. Her hands were chapped and red.

This was the kibbutz she had chosen, after much deliberation. Her work consisted of long days of laundering and working in the kitchen.

She'd had such high hopes the previous summer, after finishing two years at the agricultural school. Before graduation, she and Miriam toured the countryside together, visiting various kibbutzim to decide where they would settle and put their training to use.

Their trip began with a one-week seminar at Kibbutz Gesher, where they learned the principles concerning life on a kibbutz. Members worked without individual pay — any money earned was contributed to a common treasury. Members governed themselves, making their own rules and laws. Each kibbutz had its own distinct personality and goals toward which its members were striving. Hannah and Miriam carefully looked over the communities. They wanted to choose the kibbutz that was right for them.

Senesh decided against Gesher right away. It was located two hundred meters below sea level; the heat was tremendous. Although she didn't flinch at harsh climates, she felt the heat would sap her strength. She wouldn't be able to do anything beyond daily work and she planned to accomplish more with her life.

Next she visited a kibbutz whose members were Hungarian. While she enjoyed talking to people from her old homeland, she did not feel they were sincerely committed to building a new country. They seemed to prefer the comforts of a European life. Senesh had not come to Palestine to search out people from her past — she came to create a new life for herself.

She toured a few more kibbutzim, followed by a week-long poultry course in Jerusalem. Back at Nahalal, she delivered the valedictory speech to her graduating class. Then it was time to pack and leave. She did not mind leaving the school — she had always thought of her two years there as a training period, nothing more. But she would miss her roommates, especially Miriam.

Miriam was the only person in whom Hannah felt she could confide. They viewed the world in the same way and thought the same things were funny. A shared glance could set them off in fits of giggles. They also sparred verbally with each other, squaring off on opposing sides of an issue. Frequently their arguments lasted past curfew, until either Pnina or their neighbors yelled at them to shut up.

The other women in her class had already decided on a settlement. Not Hannah. She believed fate would step in and direct her to the place that needed her the most. ". . . I'll find the answer when the time comes," she wrote in her diary, just before leaving Nahalal in September, 1941.

She travelled to more kibbutzim the month of September, narrowing her choices down to Ginosar and Sdot-Yam. She would spend some time working at each on a trial basis before making her final decision.

She went to Sdot-Yam first. The name of the kibbutz meant "Fields of the Sea." The group was based temporarily near Haifa, but planned to move soon to a new permanent location at Caesarea, an ancient seaport twenty-two miles south. Senesh liked the idea of joining a group that was just forming. The other settlements seemed too well established. Recalling the hard work of the first pioneers, she was eager to build a community from scratch, as her predecessors once did.

She was given a taste of hard work right away, assigned to the kitchens, cooking for 80 people. A small group was at Caesarea, making the site ready for the transition. Conditions at Sdot-Yam were crude — a few wooden huts surrounded by tents. Sdot-Yam had none of the modern facilities the students had enjoyed at Nahalal. The work at the girls' school had been difficult, but at least they had proper equipment. Here it was a struggle to maintain daily living, much less build a new community.

But the people who had been working for nearly five years to create Sdot-Yam had a vision of carving out a community from the sea. Senesh believed in their project, though she realized she would be doing only menial jobs the first few years. Much of her training at the agricultural school would be wasted — Sdot-Yam would be supported by the sea, not by orchards and fields.

In October Senesh attended the Water Festival at Caesarea and saw the new site for the first time. She stood on the beach with the other members as they celebrated the drilling of the first freshwater well. Fresh water meant the group could soon move to Caesarea and begin building.

She was struck by the beauty of the place. Originally a Roman port city, Caesarea was named for the Emperor Augustus Caesar and ruled by King Herod in 22 B.C. When Jerusalem was destroyed by the Romans, Jewish captives were sent to Caesarea to be executed. In the twelfth century, Caesarea was conquered by the Crusaders, who built a fort on top of the Roman ruins.

The fortress rose from the sea like a city in a dream, waves dashing against the stone pillars. Ancient seawalls disappeared into the dunes like history being swallowed by time. The Mediterranean sparkled in the sun. Senesh fell under the spell of Caesarea's wild beauty, impressed by the weight of its past. Later she wrote a poem about Caesarea. The last lines reflected her commitment:

> *We return. We are here.*
> *Soft answers the silence of stone.*
> *We awaited you two thousand years.*

When her trial period at Sdot-Yam was up, she went to Ginosar, as planned. This group was running fairly smoothly. All the hard, interesting work had been done. Senesh stayed the month of November, knowing that she would ultimately choose Sdot-Yam. The tasks assigned her at Ginosar — working in the laundry, kitchen duties, gardening — were too easy. She wasn't using her abilities. Perhaps at Sdot-Yam, she would.

In December, 1941, she returned to Sdot-Yam, this time as a candidate. She had left most of her clothes and personal possessions with the Krausz family in Haifa. She didn't need fancy dresses to work the docks or to mend fishing nets. She was anxious to prove to the group that she was not a spoiled, rich girl, that she was willing to do more than her share.

But even with that admirable attitude, Senesh did not fit in with the people at Sdot-Yam. For the first time, she was not popular within a group. Although they accepted her, the others kept their distance. Senesh had liked the fact that the members of Sdot-Yam were mostly sabras, poorly educated and gritty. She had turned down the offer to join the Kibbutz Maagan, the Hungarian settlement, because she wanted to be with people who were different. But the differences, she soon found, were too great.

It was difficult to get to know people, for one thing. Everyone was so busy, they only had time to chat at meals. When they did talk, Senesh realized she had very little in common with them. Few were interested in things that interested her — culture, ideas, literature. When she spoke up in meetings, she was afraid the others thought she was a show-off.

She began to withdraw into herself, spending her free time reading and writing. Besides her diary, she wrote a few poems and a play called *The Violin*.

Writing wasn't easy either. She worked from six in the morning until six in the evening. By the time supper was over, she was too tired to think, much less write. The winter of 1941–1942 was cold and rainy. Senesh lived in a tent that threatened to blow down in the howling wind. Sand covered every surface. After hours of washing clothes in cold seawater, Senesh's fingers were too numb to hold a pen. She wrapped rags on top of rags in an effort to keep warm. "It's hard to imagine spring and sunshine will come again," she wrote soberly in her diary, January 2, 1942.

In the middle of the dreary winter, Miriam came to visit. They talked for hours and Hannah read her a poem she had written during her Ginosar stay. It felt so good to talk to someone who really understood her!

She seemed to be permanently assigned to the laundry. Once she was even hired out to wash clothes in a private home, an eight and a half-hour stretch of grueling labor. Senesh was proud that she was able to do "the meanest of all forms of housework," but still — wasn't there more to life than washing socks?

In February she went back to the Caesarea site and was once again enchanted with the ancient fortress by the sea. She ambled along the beach, watching waves crash on the shore, and realized the challenge ahead, wresting the land from the sea, wind, and sun. If only she could be transferred to Caesarea and do *real* work . . . but she had not yet been appointed as a full member of Sdot-Yam.

Hannah often thought of her mother and George. Catherine Senesh used to write regularly, but now letters came sporadically. From George she heard nothing at all. On the days there was no mail for her, she felt despondent. When she did receive a letter, she was still upset. Her mother would joke that her hair had turned gray, but that she was fine otherwise. Senesh suspected her mother was sparing her the truth. What was happening in the rest of the world while she was bent over her washtub?

In April, 1942, she wrote in her diary:

> Yesterday I received a letter from home. It's so difficult. . . . I've given considerable thought to enlistment.

The British army was actively recruiting in Palestine, as the war was drawing closer. Both men and women could join, though the women had to have no family connections.

Palestinian ties with the British went back many years. The British had legally governed Palestine ever since the end of World War I. Great Britain had supported the Zionist movement and was approved by the League of Nations in 1922 to rule over Jews and Arabs until Palestine's future status was determined. The British Army was based in Palestine to keep peace in the land. In the 1930's, more and more Jews fled to Palestine to escape anti-Semitic restrictions and the threat of war. In March, 1939, the British, in an effort to control growing hostilities between the Arabs and the new Jewish settlers, passed a law known as the White Paper. The White Paper limited Jewish immigration, at a time when Jews most needed a refuge.

But the Jews came anyway, some as part of the

regular quota, like Senesh, others illegally, risking their lives. In late 1941, a ship carrying over 700 illegal Jewish refugees managed to elude the Nazis, only to be halted at Istanbul. The ship was refused an entry permit to Palestine, and the Turkish government would not let the passengers disembark. For two months the *Struma* lay at anchor in the Istanbul harbor while the issue was debated. Finally the *Struma* was turned away. Two days later, the ship sank. Only one passenger survived.

The *Struma* incident angered Palestinian Jews. Senesh wrote in her diary that she was afraid war against the British was inevitable. Later, when she was at Sdot-Yam, she became familiar with the *Haganah*.

The Haganah was originally formed in 1920 as the Jewish branch of the British Army. After the war, the British did not want the Palestinians to have weapons or maintain their own self-defense, but the Haganah continued to exist without official recognition. Many members of Sdot-Yam belonged to the Haganah. They helped smuggle Jews off ships that had stolen into the port of Haifa under a cover of darkness. Senesh sometimes participated in these late-night sessions, feeding the refugees, and hiding them on the beaches while British soldiers searched the docks.

It was hard to believe that two groups with such opposite goals as the British Army and the Haganah would ever get together for a joint mission. The British needed escape routes opened in Nazi-occupied countries to rescue shot-down Allied pilots. The British also wanted to help the resistance fighters, isolated bands of men and women who were fighting their own private war with the Nazis on their home soil. The resistance fighters aided Allied pilots and acted as spies for the Allies. When the British realized they needed better information from German-occupied countries, they listened to the Haganah, who had earlier proposed a Jewish rescue mission made up of Palestinian Jews. The Jews of Palestine were dedicated to the cause, the Haganah argued, and most importantly, they spoke the native languages. A team of Jewish soldiers would be very useful to the British.

In May, 1942, Senesh was elected to Sdot-Yam's recruitment committee, and later proposed as a candidate to the *Palmach*, a secret Palestinian army. "I don't know whether I'm suited to this work," she confided to her diary, "but I'll see."

During this time Senesh read several books. One was *Gone With the Wind*. She identified with the heroine, Scarlett O'Hara, who, when faced with a crisis, would say, "I'll think about that tomorrow." Hannah wavered between periods of feeling useful to times when her life had no meaning whatsoever. She wrote of her aimlessness in her diary:

I live here like a drop of oil on water, sometimes afloat, sometimes submerged, but always remaining apart, never mixing with another drop.

In the fall of 1942, Senesh was formally accepted

as a member of Sdot-Yam. Immediately she applied for a transfer to the Caesarea settlement. Her transfer was approved in November. The news left her confused, not joyful. Although she was desperate for change, she wasn't sure she'd find her place at Caesarea, either. "I don't have a clear picture of what I'll do," she wrote halfheartedly in her diary, "but I'll do my best at whatever it turns out to be."

The war had advanced into Russia. Some of Hitler's soldiers were Hungarian men and boys, forced to fight for a cause they did not endorse. Tens of thousands of people were dying every day, while Senesh washed socks and peeled potatoes.

Then, suddenly, what she had to do came to her.

On January 8, 1943, in a departure from the previous listless diary entries, she wrote:

I've had a shattering week. I was suddenly struck by the idea of going to Hungary. I feel I must be there during these days to help organize youth emigration, and also to get my mother out.

On fire with enthusiasm, she went to Tel Aviv and Jerusalem, trying to obtain the necessary documents to go home. But the enormous difficulties of such a mission during a world war were overwhelming. She returned, discouraged, but was not about to give up her dream.

Senesh was elected storekeeper at Caesarea, responsible for obtaining food and supplies for the fledgling settlement. The job meant nothing to her. She floated through days, never mixing with others, now by choice. Parties and sing-alongs got on her nerves. How could people sing when others were dying? How could they just *sit* there? Maybe they believed it would do no good to fight, that the problems were too big for individuals to solve.

In her diary she quoted a sentence from a book she had read, *Broken Grindstones*. " 'All darkness can't extinguish a single candle, yet one candle can illuminate all its darkness.' " Maybe one person *could* make a difference. She would get to Hungary, somehow.

Then her prayers were answered.

In February, 1943, a man came to see her in Caesarea. His name was Yonah Rosen. Senesh had met him at Kibbutz Maagan, the Hungarian community. Rosen told her of an organization starting up, a group of volunteers with the same desire she had, to rescue Jews from behind enemy lines.

Apparently many Palestinian Jews were sick of picking oranges while their families in Europe suffered. Rosen outlined the basic plan: groups of Jews from various European countries would be dropped behind enemy lines into their former homelands. The mission would be supported by the British, who would supply planes and equipment.

Rosen had volunteered for the Hungarian mission. He remembered Senesh and had come to see if she was interested. The members of the mission, he emphasized, were mostly young and inexperienced, but all possessed a fiery desire to help their people.

Senesh agreed instantly. Yes, she wanted to join.

Later, she wrote excitedly in her diary, "I see the hand of destiny in this . . ."

The mission was not going to be easy. She would have to train as a soldier. There was only one way to get into enemy-occupied territory and that was by parachute.

The dangers did not matter. The only thing that mattered was the chance to help fellow Hungarians and her mother.

The distant lights that beckoned her suddenly seemed within reach.

THE BURNING FLAME
1944

8
The Mission

After Yonah Rosen had left her tent that day in February, promising he'd get in touch with her soon, Hannah Senesh was on fire to start the mission. "I can't sleep at night," she wrote in her diary. Weeks passed and still she heard nothing more from Rosen.

"My entire being is preoccupied with one thing: departure," she wrote at the end of May, 1943. "I am waiting to be called. I can't think of anything else." Mechanically she performed her duties at Caesarea, detaching herself from the other members. Just as she had once felt her spirit had flown ahead to Palestine while her physical being remained in Budapest, now she was mentally on the mission, already planning what she would say to her mother when she arrived.

When the settlement gave its permission for her

to enlist, Senesh was called to Tel Aviv to be interviewed by the British Army and members of the Haganah, the secret Jewish self-defense organization. She was aware she would have to deal with both in order to reach her goal to rescue fellow Hungarian Jews and bring her mother safely to Eretz Israel.

While Senesh waited to hear from Yonah Rosen through the spring and summer of 1943, the British and Haganah strove to reach an agreement. At last it was decided: 32 Palestinian Jews would be trained to parachute into various occupied countries to help the downed pilots, set up communication networks for the resistance fighters, and *if they had time*, rescue the Jews.

In June of 1943, Hannah Senesh was interviewed by a committee of British and Haganah officers. Knowing what the British wanted to hear, she parroted the objectives of the mission. The last goal was her first — and only — priority.

She was accepted. In December, she was summoned to Ramat Hakovesh, the kibbutz near Tel Aviv where she would receive basic training. Although the mission was under British command, the Haganah were responsible for the first two phases of training: basic combat training and the parachute course. The third part of training, intelligence, would be conducted by the British.

She arrived at Ramat Hakovesh, wondering if she would pass the training course. There were two other girls in the group, Chaviva Reik, and Sarah Braverman. Hannah Senesh had celebrated her twenty-second birthday at Caesarea that summer, and her fourth anniversary in Palestine that fall. In one of her last diary entries, she admitted she still vividly remembered the figure of her mother standing on the platform as her train slowly pulled out of the station. Senesh deeply felt the pain of separation.

Hannah Senesh was not the same girl who had happily picked olives four years before. The war had hardened her. Throughout her training she was efficient as always, but a new defiance seeped into her personality. She learned judo, practiced with knives, and mastered firearms. The firearms ultimately got her in trouble.

One day the members of the Jewish team were taking apart and reassembling their weapons, blindfolded. They had trained with Sten guns, Tommy guns, German Schmeissers, and .45 Colt automatics, mostly stolen from the Germans.

Suddenly British jeeps and trucks screeched into the training ground. As the British soldiers raided the small store of weapons, their instructor warned the team members not to resist. But Hannah Senesh was not about to let the British take away her gun.

She was hauled to her feet by two British soldiers. Struggling and protesting, she was arrested and spent two days in jail. Being reprimanded for fighting back did not diminish her passion for the mission. If anything, it made her angrier.

After successfully passing basic training, the members of the mission were sent to Ramat David, near Nahalal, where they would learn to be parachutists. Because of the time crunch, the 21-day course was cut to 10 days. There were four men in Senesh's group, all around the same age. Hannah Senesh was the only one who did not seem terrified to jump from the DC-3 Dakota. They jumped five times in five days, including one night jump.

Actually she *was* apprehensive, but she had learned to mask her fears. Like the others, she worried that her chute might not open, that she might hit the side of the plane upon jumping, that she might hit the ground too hard. But this was the only way she would be able to get into Hungary. She passed the parachute training course, but Sarah Braverman did not. Now there were only two women, Hannah Senesh and Chaviva Reik, on the mission team.

In January, 1944, Senesh returned to Caesarea to pack her things. She stored her father's books, her poems, and the notebooks containing her diary in a suitcase and left the suitcase with the kibbutz secretary until she returned.

Before turning in the suitcase, she penned her final diary entry:

This week I leave for Egypt. I am a soldier . . . I want to believe that what I've done, and will do, are right. Time will tell the rest.

She never wrote in her diary again.
Hannah Senesh left the ancient fortress by the

sea and went to Tel Aviv to await orders. It was there she met Yoel Palgi.

Yoel later wrote about their first meeting in his acount of the mission. He walked into a mission member's house and saw a woman in a British Royal Air Force uniform. She looked at him with eyes that matched the blue-gray of her uniform. He was instantly charmed by her smile.

"You're Hannah!" he said. He had heard of her. Hannah Senesh was a well-known member of the mission team.

Yoel Palgi told her he was on his way to the parachute training course. He was not looking forward to it.

Sensing his nervousness, Senesh told him it was nothing. "You go up in a plane, you jump, and you're right back on the ground," she said casually.

Palgi left in better spirits, cheered by this unusual woman. When he came back, after passing the parachute course, he invited Senesh out. They strolled around the city, ate in cafés, and took in shows. Hannah Senesh enjoyed Yoel Palgi's company. They laughed and talked and tried not to think about the journey that lay ahead. They were both tense about leaving Palestine, the land they had come to love. She told him she had a mother in Budapest and a brother in France. She worried that they would arrive in Palestine and she wouldn't be there to help them adjust.

On the day they were to leave for Cairo for the last phase of their training, Senesh received an astonishing message.

Her brother George was in Haifa. His ship had just come in and she was leaving! She burst into tears.

Palgi knew how much this meeting meant to her. He bought tickets to Haifa and arranged a 24-hour postponement. Cairo could wait a day, but Senesh could not miss seeing her brother.

In Haifa they found George Senesh in Atlit, the camp where immigrants were detained as long as two weeks. In their British Air Force uniforms, Yoel Palgi and Hannah Senesh were able to get him out of the camp early. Palgi left brother and sister alone.

George Senesh was surprised to see his little sister wearing a uniform. But she could not tell him anything.

They walked over to a cafe, where George told Hannah his incredible story.

When France fell in June 1940, George Senesh was in his second year at the textile school. He stayed long enough to graduate and took a job while waiting for his Palestine certificate. The situation for Jews in France was worsening, and he realized he would have to escape. With forged papers, George managed to cross the Spanish border in December, 1942. He was caught and imprisoned. Months later, he was freed. He moved to Cadiz, where he played Ping-Pong with a Chinese ambassador and resumed his wait for his immigration certificate. In January, 1944, while Hannah was packing her things at Caesarea, George boarded the ship *Nyassa* and left for Palestine.

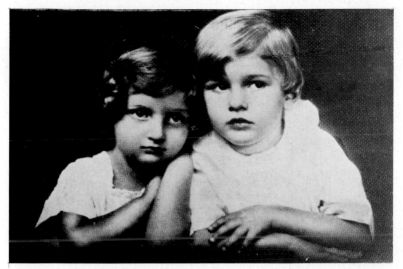

Hannah Senesh, age 3, with her brother, George, age 4.

Hannah's parents, Catherine and Bela Senesh, in 1925.

Hannah's parents and grandmother, Fini Mama, in 1926.

*Hannah, George, and their mother after the death of
Hannah's father, in about 1928.*

*Hannah,
fourteen years old.*

Catherine and Hannah Senesh.

Hannah, about sixteen years old.

At Dombovar,
summer of 1939.

At the Agricultural School in Nahalal, in 1939.

In Palestine on a day off.

Members of the Kibbutz Sdot-Yam; Hannah Senesh is in the second row, fourth from the left.

Hannah Senesh, in uniform, with her brother just before she left for the mission in February, 1944. It was their last meeting.

*Hannah Senesh's coffin being moved from Hungary
(above) to Israel (below), in 1950.*

Now here he was. And his sister was leaving. She couldn't tell him where, or when she'd be back, or even what she was doing.

She handed him a letter she had written and left with her old roommate, Miriam, to send to George should he arrive while she was gone. When she'd heard he was actually in Palestine, she had retrieved the letter from Miriam.

George read the typewritten pages. His sister talked about life in the Land, but with the attitude that she was never coming back. He was puzzled, especially when he read the postscript at the bottom, "I wrote this letter at the beginning of the parachute training course."

Senesh took the letter from him and put it back in her pocket. It was all she could reveal of her mission. She hoped he understood.

They strolled around the city. A sidewalk photographer snapped their picture.

Weeks later an envelope arrived in the mail at Kibbutz Maagan, where George Senesh was working. Inside was the photograph taken that day. Hannah, her arm linked with his, gazed up at him as he smiled into the camera.

By the time George received the photograph, Hannah Senesh was in Cairo, finishing up her intelligence training. She had learned Morse code, how to operate a radio transmitter, to read maps, forge documents, and techniques to mislead the enemy, in case they were captured.

She was impatient to begin the mission. For the Jews of Hungary, time was running out.

9
"Blessed Is the Match"

The meeting with her brother had left Hannah Senesh energized. Her upbeat mood carried over into the last part of her training. In the jeep on the way from Tel Aviv to Cairo, she suddenly declared she wanted to drive.

In his account of the mission, Yoel Palgi clearly remembered the incident. He and the three other mission members in the car pointed out that she didn't know how to drive. Unfazed, Senesh replied that it was a good time to learn.

The driver good-naturedly let her have the wheel and soon they were barreling across the Egyptian desert. Palgi covered his eyes whenever they passed another car, but Senesh handled the jeep as if she'd been driving all her life.

In Cairo she aced the intelligence training course. Her attention to detail captured the notice of a Yugoslavian instructor named Reuven Dafne. He was astonished by her total commitment to the mission. She urged Dafne to join the mission, arguing that his knowledge of Yugoslavia would be invaluable.

Only Senesh seemed certain the mission would be a complete success. The others could not hide their doubts. She bolstered flagging spirits, cheered the anxious, and held one-person pep rallies. Her attitude swung from lighthearted enthusiasm to intense dedication to their cause. In his postwar account of the mission, Reuven Dafne described her moods: "One moment she would be rolling with laughter, the next aflame with the fervor of the mission."

But when the actual departure was delayed day after day, week after week, Senesh became belligerent. Rumors eddied around headquarters that the Germans were on the verge of taking over Hungary and Romania, countries where the first two teams were headed. The British, who commanded the mission, held off, waiting to see what would happen, and trying to collect more information.

Senesh loudly voiced her objections to the endless delays. As Palgi wrote: "Hannah was the chief rebel. And she was not always right . . . She was totally unconcerned about her own safety."

On March 10, the team was ordered to get ready. Because it was too risky to be dropped directly into Hungary, the Hungarian team would parachute into Yugoslavia. Yugoslavia bordered Hungary, and the Partisan fighters—the underground army—had been operating behind enemy lines for a long time. The Hungarian team could benefit from their experience.

But first they flew to a town in Italy where the Allies maintained an air base. It was there that Reuven Dafne learned that his older brother and father had been taken to Dachau, the notorious concentration camp.

At last the announcement came: they would leave for Yugoslavia the next day.

Four members of the team — Hannah Senesh, Reuven Dafne, Yonah Rosen, and Abba Berdichev — would be dropped first. The other two members, Yoel Palgi and Peretz Goldstein, would parachute in at a later date.

At Brindisi airport, Reuven Dafne noticed the sensation Hannah Senesh created when she walked onto the airfield. Soldiers gawked when they realized one of the four about to leave on a dangerous mission was a woman. An American paratrooper came up and wordlessly shook her hand. Senesh turned her dazzling smile on him. "I can't believe it!" a Scottish sergeant exclaimed as he helped the members into their parachute harnesses, Dafne later recalled.

The team wrote final letters home while their plane was fueled and loaded. Senesh used this time to write to Sdot-Yam, since the members there had originally given her permission to go on this mission.

"On sea, land, in the air, in war and in peace,

we are all advancing toward the same goal," she wrote.

In her letter home, she wrote simply, "Mother darling, In a few days I'll be so close to you — and yet so far. Forgive me, and try to understand. With a million hugs — "

Then it was time to take off. The team members made last-minute preparations. They wore weapons under their heavy winter uniforms — in mid-March, it would be cold in Yugoslavia. Their equipment included a radio. Once set up, the radio would be used to communicate with the Partisan fighters and downed Allied pilots. They also had a radio codebook, compasses disguised as buttons, oiled silk maps (paper maps would disintegrate in bad weather), and a photograph of their squadron leader to show the Partisans as proof of their identity. After months of fighting pockets of Germans in woods and villages, the Resistance fighters were wary of strangers.

The mood suddenly turned serious as the Hungarian team boarded the plane. The cabin was jammed with supplies. They sat among boxes, weighted down by their harnesses, packs, and weapons. Senesh and Dafne would jump first. Berdichev, Rosen, and a British officer accompanying the team would jump on the second pass.

The plane took off into the night. Hannah Senesh had made only one practice jump from a night flight. This would not be practice.

She attempted light conversation but it was impossible to be heard over the roar of the engines. Dafne looked over at Senesh's glowing face. She smiled and winked. ". . . her luminous smile reminded me of a little girl on her first merry-go-round ride," he wrote later.

Exhausted with tension, the team members dozed, awaking some time later to find the crew tossing boxes attached to parachutes out of the hatch. Below, fires marked their target. The partisans were waiting for them. The dispatcher told Senesh and Dafne to get ready. They got into position by the opened hatch.

Dafne jumped first. When it was her turn, Hannah Senesh did not hesitate. She jumped fearlessly into the night.

Because she was so small, her chute carried her off course. She landed in a tree, the lines of her parachute snarled among the branches. With her knife, she freed herself and dropped to the snow-covered ground.

The Partisan fighters found her. They wore makeshift uniforms, a German coat might be paired with Italian trousers, much mended and patched. Though they looked like a ragtag army, they were professional fighters. Nearly a quarter of a million Yugoslavs had joined forces against the Germans.

They led her through the moonlit forest to a camp hidden in the trees. Dafne, Berdichev, and Rosen were waiting for her.

Two days later, they were in the Partisan headquarters. The commander of the Resistance fighters seemed fascinated by Senesh. Nearly every band of Partisans counted a woman among its ranks, so it was not unusual to see women in that region. What was unusual about Senesh was her immense confidence. In any crowd, Hannah Senesh stood out.

The General gave the Hungarian mission bad news. Hungary was now occupied by the Germans, he told them. It would be impossible to cross the border now.

Senesh burst into tears. Later, in his account of the mission, Dafne described what they were all feeling: "What will happen to all of them . . . to the million Jews in Hungary? They're in German hands now — and we're just sitting here . . . just sitting."

Senesh did not want to wait until it was safe to cross the border. She cared nothing for her own safety, only for the mission. She argued with Dafne, but he would not give in. The mission depended on the expertise of the Resistance fighters and could not cross without their help. They had no choice but to sit tight.

The Hungarian mission was entirely dependent upon the Partisans. During the day, they wandered the forests and fields with the rebel bands; at night, they slept in stables or out in the open. The Partisans had one goal — to reclaim their land from the Germans. Like the British, they were not particularly interested in helping the Jews. They only wanted to defeat the Germans. The members of the Hungarian mission were passed from one group of Partisans to another as the weeks dragged on. They hiked miles each day, avoiding German patrols. Germans controlled the valleys and major roads. The Partisans were only safe in the high mountains, where the terrain was too rugged for the German troops.

March melted into April. Mountain snow began to thaw, causing the roads below to flood. The Hungarian mission trudged behind the ox-drawn carts the Partisans used to haul their supplies and ammunition, mud caked to their knees.

During brief rest stops, Hannah Senesh wrote to her brother in Palestine. She couldn't tell him where she was or what she was doing, only that she was well and hoped he was adjusting to the hot climate. "Any news of mother?" she asked at the end of one letter. Perhaps her mother had received her immigration certificate and was, at this moment, setting foot in Haifa.

She grew more impatient every day their crossing was delayed. When Yoel Palgi and Peretz Goldstein were dropped into Yugoslavia, Palgi noticed right away that Hannah Senesh was not the same woman he had met in Tel Aviv. She was thinner, due to daily marches and the rough existence. He remarked upon other, more subtle changes: "Her eyes no longer sparkled. She was cold, sharp, her reasoning now razor-edged; she no longer trusted strangers."

One night the Partisans took the Hungarian team to a village festival. Laughter and music poured out of the meeting house. The tables were loaded with food and wine. Hannah Senesh, attracting attention as usual, was asked to say a few words. She sprang up on a table and gave the crowd one of her pep rally speeches. The room resounded with cheers. When the peasants began a wild folk dance, she joined in, quickly learning the complex steps. That night Senesh became one of the Partisans, but soon she was obstinate again, demanding that they cross the border before it was too late.

On another occasion, in a different village, the Partisans were hit in a surprise attack. German soldiers surrounded the village, firing at Partisans and civilians alike. The frightened villagers screamed in terror, clutching bundles of their belongings as shields. Bullets penetrated the pitiful piles of rags they carried and people "dropped like wounded birds," Dafne later wrote.

Dafne and Senesh became separated from the others. They ran wildly into the forest. Dafne pulled Senesh into the underbrush, where they lay gasping. German soldiers ran into the forest, too, determined to rout the Partisans who had escaped. They walked toward Senesh and Dafne's hiding place. Dafne started to pull the trigger of his rifle, but Senesh put her hand on his and shook her head. It's not worth it, her expression seemed to say. They lay there until the German patrol passed by them.

Later Dafne agreed she had been right — shooting a German in anger would have ruined the mission and endangered their lives.

May brought warmer weather. Their woolen uniforms were hot and uncomfortable.

One evening at a Partisan meeting, Dafne recognized a woman commander as a childhood friend. The woman was around Senesh's age, but looked much older. Her face was lined and her hair was almost gray. Years of fighting the Germans had left their toll. After learning the Hungarian team were all from Palestine, the woman realized they knew nothing of what was happening to the European Jews.

She told them about the roundups and deportation trains. She told them about the death camps the Jews were sent to.

They all listened, especially Hannah Senesh. She had heard stories in Palestine, but now she learned the horrible truth. A few days later, she gave Dafne a piece of paper, a poem she had written in Sardice, May 2, 1944.

By the end of May, Senesh decided she had waited long enough. She was going to cross, alone, if necessary.

Dafne was tired of wrangling with her. Reluctantly he authorized her crossing.

The poem she gave him told how passionate she felt about helping her people.

Blessed is the match consumed in kindling flame.

Blessed is the flame that burns in the secret fastness of the heart.
Blessed is the heart with strength to stop its beating for honor's sake.
Blessed is the match consumed in kindling flame.

10
The Crossing

The crossing was arranged. Reuven Dafne revived the code names they had been assigned in Cairo. He was "Geri"; Senesh was "Hagar," the name for Hungary in Medieval Jewish texts. Then they devised a key to the code using the book of French poems she would carry.

The Partisans agreed to accompany Hannah Senesh to a safe village near the border, but no farther. Their assistance did not extend into Hungarian territory; their fight was to drive the enemy from Yugoslavian soil.

Dafne had reservations about splitting the team. Uppermost in his mind was protecting the members of the mission. It was decided that Senesh would cross alone to minimize risk to the mission. If they all went at once, they might all be caught and the mission would be over. But if one crossed and was captured . . . the rest of the team was still intact. He couldn't really stop her anyway. Nothing — not even Dafne's gloomy projections — could deter her from that goal.

Yoel Palgi and Peretz Goldstein would cross the border after Senesh, opening a different escape route, and they would eventually meet her in Budapest. They set a meeting time and place: after the Sabbath service at the Great Synagogue. If Jewish services were no longer being held, then they would meet at the cathedral instead. Dafne, Rosen, and Berdichev would wait until the first group established contacts in Hungary.

As Yoel Palgi later reported, Hannah Senesh was adamant about taking some action, though she romanticized the dangers. She described an unlikely scene: the team bravely entering German-occupied forests, the woods ringing with songs of Eretz. She absolutely believed in the rightness of the mission and that they would triumph over the Third Reich.

On May 13, 1944, Senesh and Dafne began their long trek to the border that lay nearly fifty miles away. They did not know that in just two days the first Jews of Hungary would be rounded up for deportation to the death camps.

Dafne accompanied Senesh as far as the border village. He still did not like the idea of her going into Hungary with no contacts on the other side. She would be alone and virtually defenseless until she reached the city. But there was no stopping her, especially after they met the refugees.

As promised, the Partisans guided them to the border village. The journey took twenty-six days. They were forced to make long detours to avoid German patrol units. On June 9, 1944, they arrived at the village that lay a few miles from the border. The Partisans disappeared.

Senesh received her false identity papers and met a group of refugees who had just escaped from Hungary: two Hungarian Jews, Kallos and Gizi Fleischmann, and a Frenchman, Jacques Tissandier.

Using her powers of persuasion, Senesh talked the three young men who had just crossed to safety into going *back* into Hungary with her. She changed from her British uniform into civilian clothing. With her hair tied back in a headscarf, she looked like a peasant girl. Under her dress, she wore her pistol strapped around her waist. She carried a bundle of rags, which disguised her radio equipment.

As Reuven Dafne later reported, she was optimistic and laughing, cracking jokes with the British liaison officer. She told Dafne about an idea she had — when the mission was over, they would rent a big bus and travel all over Palestine as heroes, stopping at each settlement to boast of their adventures.

Shortly past seven that evening, Hannah Senesh set off with her three new companions. Reuven Dafne never saw her again.

* * *

Kallos stopped the group several times to consult his map, unsure if they had actually crossed the border into Hungary. He had risked his life to get out of Hungary and here he was going back *in*, because a determined young woman on a mysterious mission convinced him he should take her over the border.

It was getting dark. They had wandered around in circles for hours. But there was nothing to do but trudge on and hope to stumble on a landmark that would indicate they were in Hungary.

At last they came to a river. Kallos recognized it as the Drava River. Now they knew they were definitely in Hungary, but the way to Budapest lay on the other side.

For a while they walked up and down the riverbank, hunting for a bridge. There was none. They would have to swim across in the dark. Senesh sat down and opened her rag bundle, revealing the radio. Methodically she began taking it apart, as she had been taught in Cairo, then rewrapped the components in rags.

The river was icy cold and swollen from recent rains. They each had to swim with one arm, holding a piece of equipment over their heads. The strong current dragged them downstream. They fought the swift water, paddling one-handed.

Four times they swam the river, ferrying supplies and equipment. Then Senesh reassembled her radio. When Palgi met Tissandier in prison weeks later, he learned that Tissandier had urged her to leave the radio behind. He had escaped from the Germans seven times and knew that the transmitter spelled the end for all of them if they were caught with it. But Senesh did not listen to him.

They crossed three more streams that long night. By dawn the next morning, they stood on a hillside in their wet clothes, looking down at a village.

Kallos believed it was Mureska Sobatica, a town on the way to Budapest, but was not certain. It was decided that he and Fleischmann would go down to the village and inquire, while Senesh and Tissandier waited there.

Hours passed and still their companions did not return. What could be keeping them? They were only going to ask the name of the village, which was about a mile away. Something must have gone wrong.

Then they saw squads of German soldiers heading up the road toward them. They crawled through the reeds to the nearby woods behind them. They had to get rid of the transmitter — fast! Tissandier found a spot and they began digging with their bare hands. Burying the radio and their weapons, they piled dirt and leaves over the shallow grave, then scurried from the site.

Seconds before the Germans reached them, Tissandier and Senesh threw themselves into each other's arms. When the soldiers burst into the woods, Tissandier and Senesh were locked in a passionate embrace.

The officer in charge did not believe their act.

He took them to police headquarters in town for questioning.

There Hannah Senesh saw Fleischmann, beaten almost beyond recognition. He was mute with shock. Then she was taken to see Kallos. He was dead. He had shot himself in the head when he and Fleischmann were arrested on suspicion. The commanding officer produced the final piece of incriminating evidence: the radio headphones they had discovered in Kallos' knapsack.

The mission was over. It had ended right here, in a little village just inside the Hungarian border.

The officer demanded to know what she knew about the headphones. Where was the rest of the transmitter?

Hannah Senesh refused to tell them anything.

From that moment on, she was relentlessly interrogated and tortured. She was beaten on the soles of her feet and her palms with a rubber hose. Blows rained on her until she blacked out and was slapped awake. But she did not talk.

Then the commanding officer brought in the radio transmitter she and Tissandier had buried. She learned the soldiers had thoroughly searched the woods and fields around the village, destroying the village's entire corn crop in the process. But they found what they were looking for, near where they had picked up the "lovers." Now there was no denying Senesh's connection with the radio.

After two days of beatings, she was put on the train to Budapest, escorted by German guards.

Fleischmann and Tissandier were also on the train, in different cars.

Months later, Senesh told Yoel Palgi about the arrest. Handcuffed, she mulled over her situation. She knew that in Budapest they would torture her until she revealed the secret code. She recognized her own weakness. If they continued to beat her, she would eventually break and reveal the code. Then the Germans could broadcast false information to the British, and lure Allied pilots into deadly traps. Without the code, the radio was useless to the Nazis.

Senesh was sitting quite close to the train's door. The chance might not come again. She leaped up and lunged for the door. With her shoulder, she shoved it open and was about to dive from the speeding train when firm hands jerked her back.

Her guard threw her down in her seat. He told her she had no right to kill herself, she was state property. When the state was through with her, they would do away with her.

She had one recourse. The Germans had let her bring the book of French love poems, never suspecting the volume contained the very code they sought.

Working the book out of her pocket, Senesh let it drop to the floor. She kicked it under the seat, out of sight.

The train hurtled through the countryside, where Senesh had spent long summer days with her cousin Evi.

She did not know that earlier another train had

carried Evi and hundreds of other Jews, packed into cattle cars without food or water. Many had suffocated; others died of thirst or from injuries inflicted by the SS guards who had forced them into the cars. Their destination: Auschwitz, the Polish death camp.

11
Capture

At the Budapest Railway Station, Hannah Senesh was prodded into a car by guards and driven to the Horthy Miklos Street Military Prison.

Sergeant Rozsa, the tall interrogator, announced she was a traitor to her country and demanded to know who she was.

But Senesh would only give him her RAF serial number and rank. As before, her palms and the soles of her feet were beaten with a length of pipe. Her thick, curly hair was yanked out in handfuls. She was tied to a chair and whipped for hours. At one time she was smacked so hard, a front tooth was knocked out.

For hours she was tortured. Her face was so swollen she could barely see her interrogators. When her head slumped to her chest, they slapped her upright again. Blood ran into her eyes, blurring her vision, matting her tangled hair.

She had no strength left to fight. They only wanted her name. Such a small thing. What would be the harm in telling them her name? And they had promised to release her if she gave them just that little bit of information.

She told them her name.

They did not let her go. They did not stop beating her, either.

She was tossed into a cell on the top floor of the prison. The cell contained a bed and a table. On a chair sat a washbowl filled with cold water. A single slot-like window floated high above the bed.

A female guard came and removed the bowl and the chair from Senesh's cell. She was to learn that the chair and wash bowl were luxuries she was only allowed to use fifteen minutes a day.

Before she had recovered from her beating, she was hauled from her cell and dragged downstairs to a waiting police van that took her to Gestapo Headquarters. Now that the Nazis knew who she was, they wanted to know what she was doing in Hungary. Who did she know in Budapest? Who were her contacts? The questions were punctuated with more beatings. Her head lolled limply on her neck after each blow. She had told them her name and that was all she intended to say. They could kill her if they wanted, but she would not tell them about the mission.

Senesh's days became a red haze of torture and interrogation. In her cell she looked out her window by making a furniture ladder, stacking the table on her bed, and the chair on top of the table. She could see pieces of the sky and trees, a mosaic of freedom. Beyond the prison yard, she glimpsed Bimbó Street, where her mother lived.

When she heard the jangle of keys that warned her of the matron's return, she slipped off her homemade ladder and hastily set the furniture on the floor. The matron sullenly removed the chair and washbowl from Hannah's cell. In a little while, she knew, they would come for her again. It was always the same, more questions, more torture.

One day instead of the matron and the usual pair of guards, four soldiers strode into Senesh's cell. The four SS officers escorted her to Sergeant Rozsa's office in Gestapo Headquarters on Schwab Hill. She saw two people in the room: the familiar figure of Rozsa, and a woman who gripped the edge of the table with white-knuckled fingers as she stared at Senesh in utter disbelief.

It was her mother.

Catherine Senesh had been arrested that morning and brought to military headquarters. She had no idea her daughter was in the next room. When Rozsa asked her where she thought Hannah was, she told him her daughter was living on a settlement in Palestine. As Catherine Senesh later recalled in an account of her imprisonment, mother and daughter were stunned to see each other. She remembered vividly Hannah's reaction.

Senesh wrenched herself free of the guards and ran sobbing to her mother.

"Mother!" she cried. "Forgive me!"

Rozsa ordered Mrs. Senesh to make Hannah talk or they would never see each other again. Then he and the guards left the room.

Catherine Senesh was shocked over her daughter's appearance. Her eyes were black and nearly swelled shut. Her tangled hair fell over welts that striped her cheeks.

Neither spoke for a moment, overcome by emotion. Then Catherine Senesh wanted to know if Hannah had returned to Hungary for her. Senesh shook her head and said it had nothing to do with her. She added she couldn't tell her anything. It was best if her mother did not know.

Then her mother noticed her front tooth was missing. She asked if the tooth had been knocked out by the guards. Senesh said no.

In a rush of tenderness, Mrs. Senesh leaned forward to kiss her daughter. At that moment Rozsa and the guards exploded into the room.

Rozsa accused them of whispering, which was not allowed, and said they had been together enough that day.

Hannah Senesh was taken back to her cell. She did not know what would become of her mother. The Nazis had tracked down the one person who mattered most to their prisoner. Now they had the ultimate weapon to use against her: her mother's life.

Every day Senesh was jerked from her cell to a car waiting downstairs and driven to SS Headquarters on Schwab Hill. She had a new interrogator, a Gestapo officer named Seifert. He was the exact opposite of the ranting Rozsa. Captain Seifert questioned Senesh politely, even deferentially, as if he were more interested in her welfare than the information she could give him. The torture became less brutal, more calculated.

To Seifert's ceaseless questioning, she mindlessly replied she knew nothing.

More than the torture, Senesh despised solitary confinement. She hated being locked away, having no contact with the other prisoners or anyone beyond interrogators and jailors.

She paced her cell, until its cramped dimensions formed into a poem.

One — two — three . . . eight feet long,
Two strides across, the rest is dark . . .
Life hangs over me like a question mark.

One — two — three . . . maybe another week,
Or next month may still find me here,
But death, I feel, is very near.

I could have been twenty-three next July;
I gambled on what mattered most,
The dice were cast. I lost.

Prisoners favored by the SS were allowed to perform duties outside their cells. They were called trustees, because they were considered trustworthy and were granted special privileges.

112

One such trusty was Hilda, a beautiful German-born woman who spoke both German and Hungarian and often did paperwork for the Nazis. One night Hilda came to Senesh's cell. She told Senesh to look out her window.

Senesh climbed up to the window on her furniture ladder. Across the courtyard, she saw a small figure standing at the window directly opposite her own. It was her mother. She was alive and in the same prison!

Her mother remembered the meeting in her account of her imprisonment. Hannah waved eagerly. Mrs. Senesh waved back. With her index finger, Hannah drew a letter in the air. She wrote slowly, spelling out, *Hello, Mother. How are you?*

Her mother wrote back, *I am well.*

Catherine Senesh, like the other Jews, wore a large Yellow Star of David. All the prisoners wore the badge prominently displayed. Hannah asked why her mother was wearing the Yellow Star.

She replied that all Jews had to wear the Star. It was the law. She asked Hannah why she wasn't wearing one.

Hannah answered she was no longer a Hungarian citizen and was not bound by the law.

By now a small crowd had gathered at Catherine Senesh's window. She was not in solitary confinement, like Hannah, but in a large cell with other women prisoners.

One of the women finger-wrote to Senesh, *You are lucky you are not branded.*

Hannah Senesh immediately sketched an enormous Star of David in the dust on her window pane. Then she heard Hilda scurrying down the corridor and knew her time was up. She climbed down from the ladder so Hilda could remove her chair. The visit had been short, but at least she knew she could communicate with her mother.

The next evening Hilda once again appeared in Hannah's cell. She motioned for her to follow.

Hannah followed her down the hall to the bathroom. Minutes later, her mother slipped into the room. Hilda remained outside the door, keeping watch.

Mother and daughter hugged for the first time in five years. Both were crying. Catherine Senesh kissed her daughter.

Hannah observed her mother's thinness. Then she spied the bandages on Mrs. Senesh's wrists and demanded to know if the guards had hurt her.

Her mother replied sadly that she had hurt herself in a moment of despair. One of her cellmates, Baroness Böske Hatvany, had found her and bound her wrists so the guards would not see.

She asked Hannah why she was in prison.

Briefly, Senesh told her that she was a Radio Officer in the British Army. She described her arrest, but would not reveal the true nature of her mission. She confessed her sorrow at having involved her mother.

Just then Hilda whispered they had to go back to their cells.

Few meetings were arranged during the next weeks. But Hannah Senesh continued to "talk" to her mother at the window. Hilda had brought her paper scraps which she cut into letters to hold up one at a time, instead of finger-writing.

One morning Hilda brought her a small parcel. Unwrapping the paper, she found a handkerchief, a sliver of soap, a sponge, and — wonder of wonders — a jar of marmalade.

It was July 17, 1944, Hannah Senesh's birthday. She was twenty-three.

The marmalade was a present from her mother. The other gifts were donated from the meager supplies of the women in her mother's cell. That afternoon, as Catherine Senesh recalled, she received a thank-you note from her daughter. Hannah especially enjoyed the marmalade because it reminded her of Palestine and she appreciated the generosity of women she didn't even know. Even in the worst of times, people were kind and decent.

Her life had been happy and interesting, Hannah's note concluded. She thanked her mother for a wonderful childhood.

For Hannah Senesh, the carefree days of girlhood must have seemed a very long time ago.

12
Prison Windows

Hannah Senesh's window became the prison bulletin board. Inmates in cells facing the courtyard waited every morning for the latest news.

Every day Senesh was taken by police van to Schwab Hill for interrogation. Joggling along in the windowless box with about forty other prisoners, also going for questioning, she learned a great deal from them. Some were political prisoners who enjoyed certain privileges, such as newspapers, books, and mail. The interrogation process, by now routine for her, was slow and time-consuming. Senesh and the others sat in the hall and exchanged news in whispers.

A few days after her birthday, she learned of the near-assassination of Hitler. She broadcast this information from her window by pantomiming Hitler's mustache, and a jerk of her hand across her neck to indicate he had almost been killed.

One morning she asked her mother if she would like to learn Hebrew. Catherine Senesh signaled back that she would. Using her cutout letters, Hannah gave her mother a Hebrew lesson every morning.

A group of political prisoners, members of the Zionist movement, occupied the cell opposite Hannah Senesh's window. She added stories of Palestine to her daily broadcast and Hebrew lessons.

Gradually her fighting spirit resurged. Encouraged by the presence of her mother and the ability to contact other people, she became her old outgoing self. Just as she needed to write poetry and keep a diary, she needed to make her views known to the world. She had to let the world know she was there, and that she wanted to help.

Ten minutes a day, the prisoners were permitted to walk around the exercise yard, which was the courtyard beneath Senesh's window. Sometimes she watched her mother marching two by two with other female prisoners.

Senesh exercised, too, occasionally with her mother's group. Because she was confined to solitary, she was not allowed to speak with the other prisoners and had to walk alone at the rear of the line. Once when she was exercising with her mother's cellmates, she decided she would speak to her mother.

Catherine Senesh was at the head of the line, while Hannah walked by herself at the very end.

The prisoners circled the courtyard. A matron stood in the center, watching them with sharp eyes. Guards aimed their rifles, ready to fire in case a prisoner should make a run for it.

Senesh stopped suddenly and pretended to tie her shoelace. The group kept walking and when Hannah got back into her line, the woman ahead of her let Hannah quietly slip into her place. Nearly everyone in the prison knew about the mother and daughter who were being kept apart. She stooped again to fumble with her shoelace, letting the column move ahead several steps. Again, the woman in front let Hannah slip into her place. In this manner Hannah surreptitiously advanced in the line. Soon she was directly behind her mother. Catherine Senesh's exercise partner smoothly stepped back, allowing Senesh to walk beside her mother.

Mrs. Senesh recorded this incident in her account of the war years. She was overjoyed to see Hannah, since meetings between them were rare, but she was afraid they would get into trouble.

Hannah told her that they were already in jail, so they might as well talk. What could they lose?

They chatted quietly the rest of the exercise period. Hannah learned that her mother had rented her house to an actress friend, a Gentile, and that was how Mrs. Senesh had managed to hang on to her property.

On another encounter in the exercise yard, her mother asked Hannah once again why she had been arrested. Hannah told her mother it was best if she knew nothing. She assured her that she had not committed a crime, that her captors were the ones in the wrong.

Of the three matrons who worked eight-hour shifts, Marietta was by far the most cruel and sadistic. When she exercised the prisoners, she stood in the center of the courtyard like a ringmaster and cracked a bullwhip over their heads, making them trot like performing ponies. All the prisoners feared and hated Marietta. Many forfeited their ten-minute walk if Marietta was on yard duty.

One morning Hannah Senesh was so absorbed in giving her mother a lesson in Hebrew, she did not hear the matron approach her door.

Marietta burst into Senesh's cell. She accused Senesh of signaling information to the enemy and threatened to tell the guards.

Without climbing down, Senesh boldly told the woman the "enemy" she was signaling was her mother, whom she had not seen in five years.

The matron did not say a word. She simply turned on her heel and stalked out of Senesh's cell. The next morning Marietta brought in a chair so Senesh could talk to her mother, and did so every morning when she came on duty. The news from Senesh's window continued.

As the summer wore on, Senesh became a legendary figure in the prison.

Beatings at the daily interrogations lessened by degrees until Hannah Senesh was no longer being physically tortured. As her bruises healed, her youthful zest returned. Her hair grew back thick and curly. She argued gamely with her captors, warning them of the punishment they would receive after they lost the war. She told them stories about life in Palestine.

After a short questioning period, the guards would light cigarettes and sit back as if they were in a coffee shop, eager to hear her stories of Palestine.

One of Catherine Senesh's cellmates informed a new inmate that the amazing young woman she'd heard about, the one who seemed to know everything, was Hannah Senesh, Catherine's daughter, and she wasn't afraid of anything or anyone.

Hannah Senesh converted prisoners to Zionism, even as they waited on benches outside the Nazi offices. She began to feel fulfilled once more. Her purpose in life was to give people hope, even in this terrible place.

On another occasion in the exercise yard, Hannah asked her mother about two children, a boy and a girl, clinging to the hands of a woman ahead of them in the exercise column. There were several children in prison, incarcerated with their mothers, but these sad little figures seemed to symbolize the plight of the Jews. Her mother replied that the Polish mother and her children had been in camps and prisons for years.

In her cell that evening, Senesh asked Hilda if she would bring her paper and something to draw with. Hilda brought a box of broken crayons, pencils, rags, as well as pieces of paper and bits of string saved from parcels sent to the prisoners.

Senesh made two paper dolls, a boy and a girl, colored with crayons, and decorated with fabric scraps. The next morning she asked Marietta if it was possible to spend some time in the cell with the children. Soon she was out of solitary and in the communal cell with the children.

The Polish children adored her. They hung on her arms, begging for stories. Senesh realized they could not read or write and set about teaching them the alphabet. The long hours locked in the dreary cell sped by as she told stories about Palestine and tales of heroic deeds her father had once told her. Adults listened, too, grateful to escape the ugliness of prison to the wonderful world Hannah Senesh created with her words, if only for a little while.

In the prison yard, she played tag with the children, chasing them until they were all breathless and giggling. The guards pretended not to notice, but Senesh's "play school" came to the attention of less tolerant SS officials.

She was put back into solitary confinement, but she continued to make paper dolls. She made ballet dancer dolls, dolls from various historical periods, dolls from famous operas, even boy and girl kibbutznik dolls. The dolls were gifts, not just to the children, but to other prisoners, even the matrons. Marietta kept Senesh supplied with paper and fabric scraps. The Palestine dolls, carrying picks and shovels, were the most popular.

Soon it was August. One morning she asked

Marietta the date and realized it was her mother's twenty-fifth wedding anniversary.

She fashioned a vase from an empty talcum powder can covered with silver foil and a tissue paper doily. A bouquet of twenty-five white tissue paper roses were glued onto straws pulled from her mattress, then stuck into holes in the top of the can. Next she made a bride doll, dressed in a tissue paper gown holding a tiny bouquet of paper roses. A poem completed her mother's present.

Another time, she made her mother a set of boy and girl paper dolls. Her mother sent a note of thanks, saying that the dolls would be her grand-children for the time being.

One morning Senesh woke to see light dancing on the wall of her cell. Gradually she realized the spheres of sunlight were Morse code! Concentrating on the flashes, she translated the message.

The sender was Yoel Palgi.

Palgi told her that he and Peretz Goldstein were in a cell three floors down. He said he had waited by the cathedral, the meeting place they had agreed upon back in Yugoslavia, for days, but was eventually caught.

Senesh obtained a mirror and waited for the sun to move to her side of the building. That afternoon she answered Yoel, delighted to find her friend alive and well.

Palgi and Goldstein were also taken to Schwab Hill for daily questioning, but never in the same van with Senesh.

Though the torture had finally ended, the questions did not. The Nazis were determined to get the radio code. Hannah told her mother she suspected Seifert was using psychology on her. Seifert did not know that she spoke and understood German. She learned a great deal of information by listening to the guards. One of the guards appeared sympathetic toward her. Taking a chance, she asked him in German how he would punish her if the decision were his to make. He declared he had never known a woman as brave as Hannah and wouldn't punish her at all.

As the days of August passed, conditions improved for Senesh. She was not taken to Schwab Hill as often and then not at all. Interrogation stopped entirely. The prisoners were heartened by news of the approaching Russian army and the victories of the Allies.

On the surface, Hannah Senesh appeared confident. Others drew strength from her unswerving belief that the war would be over soon and the Nazis would be in the prisoners' places.

One late sultry summer evening, she stood on her chair and looked out the window. She did not talk to anyone, did not broadcast news, but simply gazed at the fragment of the starless sky visible through her narrow window, framed in the dusty Star of David. A bright August moon rose over the prison rooftop.

She was totally unaware that her mother was watching from across the courtyard. From Catherine Senesh's view, the moon bathed her daughter in soft light, forming a halo around her head.

123

Catherine Senesh had no idea what Hannah was thinking but, as she later wrote, "it seemed to me her soul was mirrored in her face at that instant."

Catherine Senesh turned from her own window and cried for her daughter.

13
"Was There Ever Such a Time?"

The Germans were losing. While the Allies battered German defenses in France, the Russians advanced toward the Hungarian border.

Rumors spread through the prison like wildfire. Rules were bent; discipline was not as severely enforced. Everyone talked about being sent to Kistarcsa, an internment camp outside Budapest.

Hannah Senesh took advantage of the lax conditions to request a transfer into her mother's cell. The Nazis would not allow mother and daughter to be together, but on September 1, Hannah Senesh was moved to a communal cell on the same floor as her mother. At last she was out of solitary and was now in her mother's group in the prison yard.

Three times a day, an inmate from each cell was permitted to draw water from the tap. Senesh's cellmates let her fetch the water from the spigot, which was directly across from her mother's cell. Senesh lingered over the task, waving to her mother. Occasionally the matron let Catherine Senesh out of her cell so mother and daughter could embrace. In return for the privilege of carrying water — any excuse to leave their cells meant a great deal to the inmates — Senesh told them stories about life in Palestine and the Zionist dream for a Jewish homeland, a place where they could be truly free.

But for some, the dream of being free was abruptly shattered. On the night of September 10, lights were snapped on all over the prison. The inmates sat up, blinking against the sudden glare as guards purposefully strode into their cells.

As Catherine Senesh later reported, no one knew what was happening. She could see Polish and other non-Hungarian prisoners in the hall, crying. A Polish woman was removed from her cell and suddenly Mrs. Senesh realized the night raid was a roundup. The Jews were going to be deported to Auschwitz. The Polish woman had told Cathering Senesh and her cellmates about the death camp in Poland.

There, Jews were forced to write postcards saying, "I am well," or "Have arrived safely." The postcards were sent to reassure relatives so they would not learn the truth. Before the postcards were in the mail, the prisoners were filing into gas chambers. But news of what really went on at Auschwitz

126

had leaked out, horrible stories beyond imagining, brought back by Jews who had managed to escape.

Hitler was getting impatient with Hungary. He wanted the Hungarian Jews "dealt with." Though the Jews in the provinces continued to be deported, the Jews of Budapest were under the temporary protection of Regent Horthy, whose government was faltering under Nazi occupation. Anxious to "clean out" the jails, the Germans ruthlessly rounded up Jews of other nationalities.

In the corridor the sound of weeping became unbearable. As the victims were marched away to the harsh commands of the Nazis, the wailing became fainter, until the prison was once again silent.

Catherine Senesh later found out that several Polish women had been taken from her daughter's cell. Hannah, she learned, had hurled herself on her bed and cried. The Nazis had unwittingly chosen the perfect punishment for Hannah Senesh. Worse than the beatings, worse even than having her mother imprisoned was having to watch helpless, innocent Jews being taken away. By locking her up, the Nazis prevented Hannah Senesh from helping her people.

The next morning, September 11, Marietta told Senesh to pack her things, she was being transferred to another prison.

Yoel Palgi, who was also being transferred, remembered seeing Senesh that day. He was standing in the hall, his nose to the wall following Nazi procedure, when he spotted Senesh running down the steps, wearing a raincoat and carrying a black bag.

"She looked so young and lovely," he recalled later, " — as if she had just returned from a journey and was stepping from the train."

As she passed him, her fingers brushed his. Instantly an SS officer bellowed at them, brandishing his pistol.

They were ordered into a police van divided into separate sections, normally used for dangerous criminals. Palgi and Senesh were put into adjoining compartments. As soon as the guard closed the doors, they tapped on the partition in Morse code. Peretz Goldstein was also in the van. Three members of the Hungarian team were alive and well.

Their destination was the Hungarian Army Prison, a place where both Palgi and Senesh had been tortured. Palgi asked the guard if he and Senesh could talk. They sat down in the hall and spoke for the first time since they parted in Yugoslavia.

Palgi told her he had been in Budapest two weeks when the Nazis arrested him. He had waited for her, first at the synagogue, then at the cathedral. But she never came.

Senesh related the story of her own capture.

"Happiness and deep sorrow mingled in our talk," Palgi wrote later. "We were all too aware of the mistakes we had made; we had learned from the experience."

128

The next day the prisoners piled in the van once more. They were being shipped to different detention centers. Senesh's stop was first, the prison on Conti Street. She leaped buoyantly from the van. At the gate, she turned to smile at Palgi and Goldstein. Putting her bag down on the walk, she gave them a spirited thumbs-up sign.

The van roared off. Yoel Palgi never saw his mission teammate again.

Two days after Hannah Senesh was transferred, Catherine Senesh was sent to Kistarcsa. After months in the military prison, Kistarcsa was like a resort. Inmates could receive packages, write letters, walk around. After a few weeks, the camp closed and Catherine Senesh made her way back to her home in Budapest.

She set out to find her daughter. Her search was hampered by restrictions. Jews were not allowed to listen to the radio, make telephone calls, or ride on buses, or in taxis. They were not permitted to sit in a park or look out their windows. It was dangerous to leave the Yellow Star at home, but Mrs. Senesh found it easier to move through Budapest without the hateful badge.

Word came that Hannah was in the Conti Street Prison. Her mother managed to arrange a ten-minute visit. She took her daughter a package. No one had much to spare these days, but friends and relatives had generously contributed clothing and food.

They met in a small room with two guards present. They hugged and talked as freely as they could with the guards listening. Hannah, her mother recalled, looked well.

Senesh told her mother her case might come to trial soon and she would need an attorney.

Catherine Senesh told her daughter about the mysterious envelope her actress friend had received in her dressing room one evening. The two men who delivered it had said the envelope contained money to be used for Hannah Senesh's defense. They added that the money came from someone named Geri, who sent his regards.

Hannah's eyes lit up and she smiled happily. "Geri" was Reuven Dafne's code name. The mission team had not forgotten her after all.

Then she unwrapped the package her mother had brought. Catherine Senesh had included a small sewing kit, a memento from her daughter's childhood. The sight of her old sewing kit caused Hannah to break down. "Does this still exist? Was there ever such a time . . . a time of childhood and carefree happiness?" Hannah said.

The ten minutes were up. Catherine Senesh asked Hannah if she needed anything. Warm clothes, Hannah had replied. It was cold in her cell. She also requested books, as she was allowed to read in this prison. In particular, she wanted a Hebrew Bible.

The next week the Allies accelerated their bombing. On Saturday, October 14, Dr. Szelecsenyi, the attorney Catherine Senesh engaged, visited Hannah Senesh at the prison. He stayed several hours, as another air attack trapped people indoors and in shelters. Senesh told him her story. The attorney was impressed by her courage and later told Catherine Senesh that her daughter was braver than most men. He also informed Mrs. Senesh that Hannah probably would be convicted if her case went to trial, but that her sentence would be meaningless. When the war was over, all political prisoners would be released. Mrs. Senesh was not completely reassured. She asked what Hannah's sentence could be. Five, seven years, was his reply. But the length of her sentence did not matter.

The next morning, German tanks rolled into the streets of Budapest. Hitler was tired of Regent Horthy's foot-dragging in "dealing" with the Jews of Budapest. Horthy was finished. He surrendered the next day, October 16. Ferenc Szalasi, the leader of the Arrow Cross, the Hungarian fascists, took over. One of Hitler's henchmen, Szalasi was only too eager to deal with the last Jews in Hungary, the Jews of Budapest. He began massive roundups.

Jews were under a strict curfew. They were only allowed out on the streets two hours a day, and then only on certain days. Between the restrictions and the bombing raids, Mrs. Senesh was unable to visit Hannah in prison. But she crept out when she could, her Yellow Star hidden by her coat, to find Hannah a Hebrew Bible. Jewish bookstores had been shut down for months, but Mrs. Senesh still had a few connections. Yet no one had a Hebrew Bible. The one thing Senesh had specifically asked for, she could not give.

From her attorney, Senesh learned of the new government and the implications it could have on her case. Now she might get ten or twenty years, even life, but the sentence still meant nothing. At no time, Szelecsenyi stressed, was her life in danger.

Her trial date was set: October 28, 1944.

14
Under Gray Skies

On the morning of October 28, 1944, Hannah Senesh was driven to the Margrit Street Prison, where her trial was to be held. A large crowd clustered around the entrance. Inside, she passed an antechamber with a sign that read "Hannah Senesh and Accomplices." She did not know that her mother, unable to attend the trial, was waiting in the little room.

The courtroom was packed. The sentencing of the female British paratrooper had garnered a lot of attention. Although there is no official record of Senesh's trial, her "accomplices," Gizi Fleischmann and Jacques Tissandier, attended the hearing and later gave their testimonies of the proceedings.

Her trial was presided over by two Hungarian judges and a Judge Advocate, Captain Simon. The

President of the Tribunal charged her with treason. He then asked her if she was guilty or not guilty of the charges.

Senesh replied that she was not guilty and requested permission to speak in her own defense.

"I do not admit treason to my native land, Hungary," she said. "I came here in the service of my Homeland, Eretz Israel."

She went on to say that she had been born in Budapest, but felt she had no place in Hungary as a Jew.

"You cancelled my citizenship with your hate," she accused. "You also raised your hand against my people. Thus it is not I who is the traitor! They are traitors who brought calamity upon our people, and upon themselves. I implore you, don't add to your crimes. Save my people in the short time it remains in your power to do so. Every Jew who remains alive in Hungary will make the judgment against you after you fall!"

Her last words fell upon a shocked silence.

Then the President declared a short recess. The judges left to deliberate Hannah Senesh's sentence.

Senesh was caught in the tide of people leaving the courtroom. Her attorney, Szelecsenyi, escorted her to the hall. When Senesh saw her mother, nervously clutching a handbag to hide her Yellow Star, she ran over and threw her arms around her.

Hannah was bubbling, jubilant, Catherine Senesh said later. She started to speak to her daughter but the guard separated them. They were not allowed to talk until the sentence had been passed.

Then Senesh was called back into the courtroom. Minutes later, she returned, elated. The judges were unable to reach a decision. Sentencing would take place in eight days, on November 4.

Catherine Senesh was worried by this development, but Szelecsenyi reassured her that although postponements were unusual, the delay had no real significance. Senesh thanked her attorney for his efforts on her behalf, as he left for another trial.

Alone with her daughter, Catherine Senesh again voiced her concern.

Hannah urged her not to worry and added that she would be detained in prison until the war was over. She noticed how her mother held her purse so that it hid the Yellow Star. Hannah asked if someone could hide her mother.

Catherine Senesh replied that she couldn't think of hiding until Hannah's case was settled.

The guard, who had let mother and daughter have a few moments alone, came to take Senesh back to Conti Street Prison. He told Catherine Senesh she could walk with them. Now that the trial was over, she was allowed to visit her daughter as often as she liked. All she needed was a visitor's pass from the prison office.

Mrs. Senesh promised Hannah she'd come see her on Monday.

At the bottom of the steps, the guard went ahead to see if the car had arrived. Senesh remarked that she wished she could go by tram, to see ordinary people, doing ordinary things. She meant she longed to be an ordinary person herself, but it was too late for that, of course.

Catherine Senesh was not permitted to walk across the lawn with them. She stood at the foot of the steps and watched her daughter disappear into the crowd that still milled around the building.

The next four days the Allies shelled Budapest with a vengeance. The Red Army was approaching steadily from the east as the Allies increased air attacks.

The prison on Conti Street was evacuated. Vanloads of prisoners were taken to the Margrit Street Prison, where Hannah Senesh had been tried. Senesh was one of the last prisoners transferred.

She was put in solitary confinement, Cell 13. Conditions at this prison had deteriorated to the point where the inmates were only given watered-down soup once a day. She was hungry and cold. The chill of November penetrated her unheated cell.

Yoel Palgi and Peretz Goldstein were also in this prison. Palgi recalled later that "confusion reigned." Senesh's judges had fled before Palgi and Goldstein were tried. The guards were busy burning records or fleeing to save their own skins. Nazi control faltered more with each bomb that dropped. The prisoners knew the war was nearly over but would they be rescued before they starved?

Alone in her chilly cell, the guns booming outside, Hannah Senesh did not know that her mother had tried to come see her every day since the trial. She did not know that air raids had forced Catherine Senesh to remain indoors several days, and when Catherine did venture out, she was repeatedly turned away from the office that issued the visitors' passes. Captain Simon, the only person who could authorize passes, was conveniently out of his office. Senesh did not know any of this, only that the hours crawled by slowly.

The morning of November 7 dawned cloudy and gray.

Palgi learned months later what had happened that day, when he met a former prison orderly in a clinic. The man had been cleaning outside Cell 13 that morning. He saw Captain Simon, the Judge Advocate, enter Senesh's cell. He heard Captain Simon tell Senesh that she had been sentenced to death and did she wish to ask for clemency?

Senesh replied that she wanted to appeal, but Simon told her there would be no appeals. He repeated his question: Did she wish to ask for clemency?

"Clemency — from you?" Senesh reportedly said. "Do you think I'm going to plead with hangmen and murderers? I shall *never* ask you for mercy."

Captain Simon told her to prepare to die. She had one hour in which to write farewell letters.

A guard brought her paper and pen. Then she was left alone.

This was it, the end of the heroic quest she had set out on months — years — ago. The remaining minutes of her life dribbled away like the grains of sand that had slipped through her fingers at Caesarea.

No one knows what Hannah Senesh thought about in that last hour. She might have thought about the green fields of Nahalal, the orange groves, the sparkling Mediterranean. She might have thought about George, who was working at Kibbutz Maagan. She might have thought about her teammates on the mission. She probably regretted the heartbreak she was about to cause her mother.

She wrote her farewell letters. Then she sat on her cot to wait.

At ten o'clock, Captain Simon unlocked the door of her cell. He gestured abruptly for her to follow him. A pair of guards flanked her as they walked silently down to the courtyard.

Although there were no eyewitnesses to the event that followed, Yoel Palgi was able to piece together what happened. After he and the others heard the shots, someone in his cell climbed up to look out the window. In the courtyard below he saw a sandbox near the prison chapel and a table with a crucifix on it. But no sign of an execution.

It is assumed the soldiers hammered a post into the sand, secured Senesh's hands behind her back, then tied her to the post.

An officer approached with a blindfold. Senesh

looked into his eyes and shook her head. She did not want to spend her last seconds on earth in darkness.

The firing squad assembled before her. She stoically faced them, chin up.

"Ready," Simon called. The soldiers shouldered their rifles.

"Aim . . ." The rifles cocked.

"Fire!"

That afternoon, one of Palgi's cellmates pretended to be sick. At the clinic he learned the meaning of the shots they all heard that morning. Hannah Senesh had been executed.

Catherine Senesh had arrived at the prison at 10:30, a half hour after her daughter's execution. Captain Simon told her coldly that Hannah Senesh had been found guilty of treason and sentenced to death. He said Senesh had written farewell letters, which he would give her later, and that she could pick up her daughter's things in a few days.

Captain Simon had taken it upon himself to have Hannah Senesh executed. There had been no sentencing. He could have been annoyed by Senesh's speech during the trial or by her very presence, always brave, never buckling under to the Nazis. To him she might have been one more trouble-making Jew. Whatever his reasons, he alone made the decision to have her killed.

Numbly Catherine Senesh went to the prison to collect her daughter's belongings. Captain Simon never gave her the letters. But in the pocket of one of Senesh's dresses, she found, written on scraps of paper, a poem and this note:

Dearest Mother:
    I don't know what to say — only this: a million thanks, and forgive me, if you can.
    You know so well why words aren't necessary.

With love forever,
Your daughter

Epilogue

The day after Senesh's execution, November 8, the long march began. Thousands of Budapest Jews were forced to walk to work camps in Germany and Austria. There weren't any trains to transport the victims, and the Allies had blocked the rail lines. The old, the young, and the sick plodded down the road, driven by Hungarian soldiers who used whips and rifle butts to keep them moving. Many died on the road from exposure, fatigue, injuries, and starvation.

Catherine Senesh was forced to join the march on November 14, 1944. Grief-stricken over her daughter's death, she trudged in the rain and cold. Signs posted along the way warned people not to help the marchers, under penalty of death. After six days on the road, Catherine Senesh escaped and returned to Budapest. With the aid of friends, she went into hiding and spent the remaining three months of the war in a convent hospital.

In April, 1945, Hitler committed suicide, and in May, Germany surrendered to the Allies. Although the war in the Pacific continued until August, the war in Europe was over.

Millions of people, including six million Jews were murdered. A half a million Hungarian Jews perished during the war.

Hannah Senesh had devoted the last months of her life to giving people hope and the strength to fight back. Her courage symbolized the heroism of people who fought against incredible odds.

After her execution, she was buried in the martyrs' section of a Jewish cemetery in Budapest. In 1950, after the establishment of the nation of Israel, her remains were transported to the land she loved so much. Her body was buried with military honors, in the Heroes' Cemetery overlooking Jerusalem. Senesh's memorial is one of seven gravestones that form a V. A parachute is engraved on each of the seven stones, one for each member of the mission who did not return. They are known as the Seven Who Fell: Abba Berdichev, Zvi Ben Jacob, Chaviva Reik, Rafael Reis, Enzo Sereni, Peretz Goldstein, and Hannah Senesh.

Hannah Senesh is a folk heroine in Israel. Monuments have been dedicated to her memory. Several streets, a ship, farming settlements, a forest, and a species of flower have been named after her. Every schoolchild in Israel can recite the "Blessed Is The Match" poem.

But perhaps the memorial that would have meant the most to Hannah Senesh was an old ship christened the *S. S. Hannah Senes*. After the war, countless Jews were left homeless. They wanted to live peacefully in a land where they could be truly free. They needed a place where they could heal. Immigration was still limited by the British, but Palestinian Jews used old ships to smuggle Holocaust survivors into Palestine.

In December, 1945, the *S. S. Hannah Senes* safely launched 250 immigrants on the Nahariya shore, after successfully dodging the British blockade. The dazed survivors of marches and raids and death camps stepped out of the dark hold and into the brilliant light of freedom.

The distant lights that had beckoned to Hannah Senesh were suddenly within reach, and glowed like a beacon, welcoming them home.

What Happened to the People in Hannah Senesh's Life

Family:

Catherine Senesh — Eventually emigrated to Israel, worked as a piano teacher at Kibbutz Maagan, then as a nursery school teacher in Haifa.

George Senesh — left Kibbutz Maagan to join the Jewish Brigade (a brigade composed of Palestinian Jews that served throughout Europe in 1944–45), married, had two sons, moved to Haifa.

Evi Sas — Hannah's cousin, killed at Auschwitz.

School:

Miriam — Hannah's roommate at Nahalal, taught at Kibbutz Hatzor, married, had children.

The Mission:

Yonah Rosen — returned to Kibbutz Maagan, married.

Reuven Dafne — became director of Yad Vashem, the Holocaust Memorial in Jerusalem, near the cemetery where Hannah Senesh is buried.

Yoel Palgi — escaped from the deportation train to Auschwitz, returned to Kibbutz Maagan, became ambassador to Tanzania.

Peretz Goldstein — one of the Seven Who Fell.

Abba Berdichev — one of the Seven Who Fell.

Chaviva Reik — the other female parachutist on Hannah Senesh's mission, was dropped into Czechoslovakia where she helped Allied pilots and Russian prisoners, was captured and executed. One of the Seven Who Fell.

Gizi Fleischmann and Jacques Tissandier — arrested with Hannah Senesh, attended her trial as accomplices, survived to give accounts of the proceedings.

Bibliography

Books

Hannah Senesh: Her Life and Diary. New York: Schocken Books, 1966.

Arad, Yitzhak, *The Partisan: From the Valley of Death to Mount Zion.* New York: Holocaust Library, 1979.

Atkinson, Linda, *In Kindling Flame: The Story of Hannah Senesh 1921–1944.* New York: Lothrop, 1985.

Bondy, Ruth, *The Emissary: A Life of Enzo Sereni.* Boston: Atlantic Monthly Press, 1973.

Cahill, Mary Jane, *Israel.* New York: Chelsea House, 1988.

Dormandy, Clara, *Hungary.* New York: Sterling Publishing Co. Inc., 1970.

Elon, Amos, *Understanding Israel.* New York: Behrman House, Inc. Publishers, 1976.

Fine, Helen, *Behold the Land.* New York: Union of Hebrew Congregations, 1968.

Golden, Harry, *The Israelis.* New York: G. P. Putman, 1971.

Gross, David, *Pride of Our People.* New York: Doubleday, 1979.

Hazleton, Lesley, *Where Mountains Roar*. New York: Holt, Rhinehart, Winston, 1980.

Hezog, Chaim, *Heroes of Israel: Profiles of Jewish Courage*. Boston: Little, Brown, 1989.

Kimche, Jon and David, *The Secret Roads*. New York: Farrar, Strauss and Gudahy, Inc., 1955.

Levin, Meyer, *The History of Israel*. New York: Putnam, 1976.

Malka, Victor, *Israel Observed*. New York: Oxford University Press, 1972.

Masters, Anthony, *The Summer That Bled*. New York: St. Martin's Press, 1972.

Purdy, Susan Gold, *Jewish Holidays*. New York: J. B. Lippincott Co., 1969.

Schur, Maxine, *Hannah Szenes: A Song of Life*. Philadelphia: Jewish Publication Society, 1986.

Volgyes, Ivan. *Hungary: A Nation of Contradictions*. Boulder, Colorado: Westview Press, 1982.

Whitman, Ruth, *The Testing of Hannah Senesh*. Detroit: Wayne State University Press, 1986.

Periodical
Wilner, Lori, "The Paradoxical Heroism of Chana Senesh." *Lilith* #20 (1988): 22–23.

Index

151

St. Michael School
1203 E. 10th Ave.
Olympia, WA 98501